Dear Inze,

Stories from the Continent, and
a lost age.

Yours,

x-Mar 2.12

The MONKEY
and other stories

Miklós Bánffy

Translated from the Hungarian
by Thomas Sneddon

BLUE DANUBE

BLUE
~
DANUBE

An imprint of Somerset Books, Budapest
Distributed by Blue Guides Limited of London
Distributed in the USA by WW Norton & Company, Inc.
500 Fifth Avenue, New York, NY 10110.

Translated from the Hungarian
English translation © Thomas Sneddon 2021.
Danse Macabre (*Haláltánc*, 1928); Lememame (*Lememáme*, 1915 and 1943); The Emperor's Secret (*A császár titka*, 1911); Wolves (*Farkasok*, 1908); The Infected Planet (*A fertőzött planéta*, 1939); Somewhere (*Valahol*, 1924); Helen in Sparta (*Heléna Spártában*, 1934); Talking Nothing (*Beszéljünk semmit!*, 1946); The Monkey (*A majom*, after 1940).

ISBN 978-1-905131-90-7

Cover: Detail from an 18th-century screen after designs by A.-F. Desportes. The J. Paul Getty Museum, Los Angeles.
Map by Dimap Bt.

Printed and bound in Great Britain by TJ Books.

 somersetbooks.com/bluedanube

Contents

Acknowledgements: I would like to thank Tom Barcsay and Michael O'Sullivan, who were kind enough to read through early drafts of these translations, and offered a great deal of useful advice. My fiancée, Zsófia Bodó, also offered invaluable help, especially when it came to the nuances of particular Hungarian words and expressions. Lastly, I should like to thank my publishers, Tom Howells and Annabel Barber. Annabel in particular, besides providing scrupulous and thoughtful editing, also played a vital role in the selection, arrangement and presentation of these short stories. Without her help, the book would have been considerably less than what it is. Any errors which remain are, of course, my own.   *T.S.*

Translator's Introduction

In May of 1935, the Hungarian literary journal *Nyugat* published a review of 'They Were Counted', the first book in Miklós Bánffy's *Transylvanian Trilogy*. The review was written by the great Hungarian novelist and literary critic Antal Szerb, author of *Journey by Moonlight* and the *Pendragon Legend*. Besides praising Bánffy's novel, he offered some astute observations:

> The first task of the critic, of course, is to say that the novel, as a novel, is outstanding—admirably surefooted composition, and altogether a first-rate read. It must also be said, however, that the style is very surprising: a sort of patrician Hungarian, employing unusual, suggestive sentence structures and lexical idiosyncrasies which are at once imposing and difficult to pin down. This is, beyond doubt, the single most significant work which Count Miklós Bánffy has produced in a long and successful career, and once more confirms that he is no mere aristocrat with a penchant for writing, but a writer who has earned his place in Hungarian literature.
>
> The middle class has, for the most part, a monopoly on literature, and [...] in the writing of aristocrats

there is almost always a certain democratic tendency, something of the 'more than a king, I am a man!' attitude, and at times even a distinctly apologetic air: 'A prince I may be, but let me venture to say this…' This impulse is entirely absent from Count Miklós Bánffy's work, and it is precisely this absence which makes the book so intrinsically interesting. Bánffy writes as a count, not merely as a writer who happened to be born a count.

There is much here which bears attending to. First, his language. It is true that Bánffy writes in a manner which was, even in his own day, entirely his own. His style is difficult to describe, and more difficult still to reproduce, but is reflected to an extent in the range of themes found in this collection. At times he writes with an earthy affinity for nature, and an almost Pre-Raphaelite impulse to capture the natural world in all its variegated, kaleidoscopic richness. As Bánffy's Romanian translator, Marius Tabacu, once remarked to me in conversation, to translate Bánffy is to become an accidental botanist and zoologist. Bánffy has a greater familiarity with, and interest in, the struggles of peasants and woodsmen of remote mountain villages than with the bourgeoisie of modern, bustling Budapest, and his membership of a family which could trace its history back through many centuries— living in a great house, Bonchida, which had been inhabited and extended by an unbroken line of Bánffys since at least the late fifteenth century—gives him a deep, instinctive grasp of pre-industrial European life which few men of letters would have possessed, even in his day.

At the same time, there is nothing either provincial or backward-looking about Bánffy's work. He was fluent in many languages, and his writings are peppered with words and phrases in English, German, French, Italian and Romanian. He was both well-travelled and well-read, and the sheer range of his interests are reflected in this collection, which spans huge reaches of time and space—once, indeed, into outer space—showing an imagination equally at home inhabiting the perspectives of a fifth-century Chinese mandarin, Helen of Troy, an eighteenth-century Swedish aristocrat, a Romanian woodsman and an eccentric Scottish diplomat.

It is worth noting at this point that the range of time periods covered in these stories is to some extent mirrored in their composition: the earliest story, 'Wolves', was written in 1908, when Bánffy was thirty-two, and the last, 'The Monkey', was written during the Second World War, when he was almost seventy. As such, and in spite of certain lifelong continuities in his interests and values, these stories should not be taken as a single, unified work, but rather as representing the changing perspectives of a complex individual living through eventful times.

Hungary's fate in the twentieth century was not a happy one, and Bánffy's life had its share of tragedy, both individually and as part of wider disasters. There is no space here for even the most cursory overview of what was, by any standards, an improbably full life and career. It is enough to say that he was born and grew up as part of Hungary's ruling elite, but ended his life as a penniless 'class enemy' in communist Budapest, exiled from the Transylvania which was his true home. What is remarkable is the way, the more insistently tragedy hems him in, the more doggedly cheerful and optimistic his fiction becomes. This refusal to wallow in despair, even as disaster looms, is curiously mirrored in the work of Szerb himself, who abandoned the mock-Gothic horror of the *Pendragon Legend* to write *The Queen's Necklace*, a charmingly light-hearted, witty account of a scandal involving Marie-Antoinette (alluded to in Bánffy's 'Danse Macabre') while war raged and Hungary's Jewish laws made his life ever more impossible.

Even so vague an attempt as this at framing Bánffy's stories must, however, remain hesitant and conjectural, for there is another key aspect to his writing which Szerb alludes to in his review, a quality he calls '*nehezen meghatározható*' and which I have translated as 'difficult to pin down'—literally 'difficult to define'. Many of these tales possess, at first glance, a superficial straightforwardness, but the more one seeks some unequivocal meaning in them, the most slippery and elusive they become. What, for instance, are we to make of 'The Infected Planet'? It feels eerily prescient, but did Bánffy intend it primarily as a warning about humanity's ecological impact or as a premonition of the cataclysmic war which, in 1939, he could clearly see approaching? And what is the relation between this strange, extra-planetary vision and the frame narrative about a shooting trip to Scotland? Such stimulating ambiguities are characteristic of these often deceptively simple stories.

Beyond this, the qualities in Bánffy's writing which most particularly strike the translator, and which I have laboured hard to convey in English, are the geniality, charm, warmth, and human sympathy which abound on every page. Some writers are simply good company, and I feel an obligation to make clear what an unalloyed pleasure it has been to work with these stories; I hope the reader finds something of this warmth and charm, and takes similar enjoyment in their English iterations.

Thomas Sneddon. Budapest, 2021

A note on place names

Some of these stories, especially those set wholly or partly in Transylvania, feature regions, towns and cities which changed hands, and thus changed names, over the course of the twentieth century. These are fraught issues, even today, and if we have chosen in the main to retain Bánffy's Hungarian designations, giving other names (largely Romanian) in endnotes, it is simply from an inclination to stick, where possible, as close as possible to Bánffy's original text, and because the stories in question are set at a time when these territories formed part of Hungary, making other designations appear somewhat anachronistic. They should not be taken as indicating any particular political stance on the part of either the translator or the publisher.

DANSE MACABRE

The Hall of Mirrors in the Palace of Versailles was not yet quite full. There was to be a ball that evening, and a steady stream of couples passed through the great doors. Unerringly they made their way to a particular point and then stopped, as though after counting a set number of paces. All stood just a hair's breadth closer to the doorway of the royal apartments than befitted their rank and favour with the king. With the utmost precision. This, after all, was the most perfect court in all Europe.

A fact hardly to be wondered at, since elsewhere in Europe the nobility had other business to attend to. They served in the army, or in the civil service, or tended their country estates, and only went to court on the grandest or most pressing occasions. In France, by contrast, the only real occupation of an aristocrat was to bask in the radiance of the king. 'I am at court,' was their continual refrain. Quite understandable, since it was here that all favour, all social and material advantage—advancement, indeed, in every sphere of life—might be obtained, though not through diligent service or natural aptitude. Instead, preferment was won through continual presence and a ready smile, and perhaps a few tricks and stratagems when occasion demanded.

But the most vital thing of all was to be vigilant. Success went to those who recognised in good time who the King's favourites were, but especially to those skilled at divining who the men of tomorrow would be and ingratiating themselves in advance.

An observer gazing down that long hall, illuminated by a thousand candles set in glittering chandeliers, each reflected over and over in the mirrored walls, would have seen a parade of gorgeously attired men with powdered hair, and women in dresses of the most fashionable colours of the day. No one who saw the many curtseys, bows and kissed hands, or heard the gracious compliments and witty remarks, could have guessed that all these fine men and women had but one thought in their minds: how they might advance themselves and ruin their rivals' reputations, winning social preferment by clambering over the backs of those whom they had destroyed.

And all was commotion, like a prodded beehive.

'It is simply monstrous that they dare write such nonsense about my sister-in-law, Her Majesty the Queen!'

These words were spoken by a decidedly plump young man with a prominent nose. He was standing next to the entrance to the royal apartments and his voice had just the right tone of indignant outrage. He was the Comte de Provence and a brother of the King, Louis XVI. As heir to the throne (the King's only child, at this time, being a baby girl) he should have been inside the royal apartments, where a procession was being organised with the royal family at its head. He had slipped out into the Hall of Mirrors, however, because he wished to cultivate an image of himself as someone who cared little for pomp and ceremony.

His satin suit, in a deep shade of taupe, had only a very modest trim of gold lace and the diamond buttons were really quite small, while the cross at his neck, of the Order of the Holy Spirit, was his only formal mark of rank. A single, carefully positioned curl fell across his heavy jowls, he held his velvet gloves nonchalantly in one hand, and wore only a single watch in his waistcoat. He attached great importance to these and many other carefully chosen details, since they showed him to be a man of simple tastes. By his dress and accoutrements he wished to suggest that he would be a modern, enlightened monarch, in touch with the democratic spirit of the age.

But this was not his only reason for coming out into the hall: he was also curious. He knew that a scurrilous pamphlet was in private circulation concerning his elder brother, and he hoped—no, he was sure!—that one of his confidantes would have all the latest news. Sure enough, an equerry in a salmon-pink coat of velvet had been waiting for just such an opportunity, and immediately hurried over to whisper in his ear.

Yes! The pamphlet had been published! How awful!

The royal censor had, of course, confiscated everything that could be found, but a few copies had nonetheless been smuggled into the capital; Paris had spoken—and laughed—about little else all day.

'Appalling!' gasped the Comte de Provence. 'And there was no way to stop it?'

'Indeed not. The royal censor paid fifty thousand *livres* to destroy the original manuscript but they say it was reprinted...well, somewhere else...'

The man in the salmon-pink coat looked into the sombre face of his patron, where only a slight glint in those watery eyes betrayed his secret delight. They were silent for a moment, then the equerry went on.

'The problem, alas, is that the pamphlet is well-written. Diverting. All the most obscene slander, of course. It states...well, it states that the child is actually your younger brother's...'

'Dreadful! Simply frightful! And to think that the Queen's charming familiarity of manner and the frivolity of my brother Charles have led to this! Alas! Oh, how it grieves me! And did the royal censor really spend so much money trying to suppress the document?'

'Indeed, Your Highness. Fifty thousand *livres*.'

'Not enough! He should have spent more!'

The plump young man's voice was full of deep distress, but then, apropos of nothing, and in an almost indecent outburst of good humour, he laughed so loudly that some of those nearby turned to look at him with surprise.

A bright procession still streamed up the marble staircase. The two rows of motionless royal guards, each of whom held a long halberd, left a space so narrow that at most two people could ascend the stairs side by side. This was quite deliberate, since only thus would there be enough time for gossip as they walked. The ladies in their stiff panniers, for all the world like upturned bellflowers, swayed slowly up the stairs, their arms outstretched so that their fingertips rested in the hand of a suitor. This too was quite in order, since noble manners in those days required that a woman should always be supported from at least one side, and perhaps two, as though she would be quite incapable of remaining upright on her own. This also afforded ample opportunity for an expressive yet discreet squeeze of the hand, or for a perfumed letter suggesting a time and place for an hour's sweet dalliance to be pressed into a gloved palm.

And so in twos and threes they glided up the stairs, each couple almost dance-like in their graceful steps.

Amid all that kaleidoscopic, chattering, smiling crowd,

only one man walked alone. He was a tall, slender youth, and his pale countenance indicated a serious, somewhat reserved character. Though his sea-grey eyes were wide open, he seemed not to perceive the crowd around him, but gazed instead at some fixed point in the distance. He always smiled distractedly if greeted by an acquaintance, but slipped away as soon as he could, letting himself be carried along.

At last he reached the top. He wanted to hurry through the Hall of Mirrors, so as to claim a seat at the front, but felt a hand grasp his arm and turned to see an elderly gentleman in black felt, who had evidently been waiting for him. The youth looked at him in surprise.

'Count Fersen,' the old man said quietly, 'I am the Queen's cabinet secretary. If Your Lordship would be so kind as to follow me.'

Without waiting for an answer he turned and set off, moving through the crowd with the noiseless, gliding steps of a man accustomed to life at court.

As soon as the old man spoke, Fersen's heart had begun to hammer in his chest. He could feel the deep blush spreading across his cheeks, and it came as a relief when they turned a corner and left the crowded gallery behind. The noise died almost to nothing as soon as the secretary closed the door behind them. They walked down the dimly lit corridor, then descended a flight of service stairs which were so dark that Fersen had to grip the iron banister and place each step with care. Along another corridor they passed two dim rooms, the walls of which were lined from floor to ceiling with cupboards. Then they came to a third room, no larger than the other two, and stepped inside. There was another door on the far side of the room, but his guide proceeded no further. Fersen looked around. The walls on either side of the fireplace were dimly lit by wall sconces. He could also make out a table, a few armchairs, and a simple bed of painted pine. That was all the furniture in the room. The bed was covered with a single sheet of coarse cloth, but he could see there was nothing else beneath it except the mattress.

'This room is used by the Queen's lady-in-waiting, when she is needed to assist in Her Majesty's toilette. Pardon me for bringing Your Lordship here, but Her Majesty wishes to speak to you alone and without witnesses. Please wait here while I announce your presence.'

Bowing deeply, he disappeared through the far door, with the same noiseless steps.

All at once Fersen was alone, and his face grew paler than ever. All the blood rushed to his heart, and for an instant he felt faint and light-headed.

The Queen!

In a sudden flood, he recalled all that had happened since the previous spring. He had been sent here by his father, Field Marshal of the Swedish army, to finish his education in manners, decorum and, *en passant*, the science of modern warfare. He was, after all, destined for a military career. He had been splendidly received at the French court and in spite of his youth, King Louis XVI had made him a colonel of the French army. This was a very great honour, especially for a foreigner, but the truth was that Fersen had hardly noticed, for ever since his arrival, his soul had been captivated, enraptured, enthralled, by a single person. The Queen. In the very moment when he was first introduced to her, he had fallen hopelessly in love.

For her part, the Queen had shown to him all signs of friendly affection. She evidently enjoyed talking to him, and he sensed that she was more open and honest with him than with the others, as though this Latin world was as foreign to her as it was to him. As though some deep affinity bound their two hearts. Soon he was part of her inner circle—that group of cheerful, light-hearted, rather superficial young people who surrounded the Queen and among whom she tried to forget the detested ceremonies of the court. This much-envied group included the King's youngest brother, Charles, Comte d'Artois; Athemar; the dukes of Lauzun and Coigny; the famously handsome Count Dillon[1]; a Hungarian by the name of Count Bálint Esterházy; and Baron Besenval, a lieutenant colonel in the Swiss Guard. In their company the year became a constant round of plays, pastoral games and masked balls, which only men of wit and cheerful good humour were permitted to attend. Fersen was admitted to this endless dance, though he was by nature a quiet, even-tempered man of few words. In their company he was like a creature from another world.

And he was happy. Endlessly, thoughtlessly happy in his hopeless adoration. He could spend every day with her. What more did he need? To see her every day, to hear her laughter and follow in her footsteps. To hold her music for her when she sang, to touch her fingertips when they danced a gavotte, or pick up a garland of flowers which she had woven and then carelessly discarded. Simply to be in her presence and occasionally, ever so rarely, to be graced with a friendly word or two. No, not merely friendly, for he detected in her voice something warmer, deeper; some chord of fellow feeling in which sounded a hidden note of truth.

That was how he had spent the year, concealing this fateful secret from everyone. And if some acquaintance was tactless enough to make some ambiguous remark about his fondness for the Queen, he always dismissed it with brusque scorn.

And now? What would happen now?

A great many thoughts rushed through his head, but not for a single instant did he imagine that the Queen might have any sort of physical liaison in mind. Perhaps she needed a trusted confidant to undertake some vital service, a dangerous task of which he could never speak a word. Might she require him to fight a duel for her? Whatever she asked, he knew he would do it, though it cost him his life.

Still he waited, as some mixture of pleasure, fear, humility and proud fidelity coursed through his veins. Motionless, he fixed his eyes upon the brass door handle, which glinted in the dim candlelight as though it were the lodestar of this new, undreamed-of, selfless happiness which welled within him.

The Hall of Mirrors, meanwhile, continued to fill with guests, including the group of young men who made up the Queen's inner circle. Coigny, who was also the King's most trusted confidant, had already arrived. Entering the hall, he had at once been engulfed by an adulatory swarm, though among the stream of flattery there were also a few sly, ambiguous references to the pamphlet, all spoken in a tone of light-hearted, mocking irony. Coigny heard them with a faint smile. He only drew himself up a little, and adopted a self-consciously mysterious expression, when one of the ladies addressed him in a shrill voice.

'The whole thing is simply absurd! The idea that that sweet little girl could be Artois' child! You, dear Coigny, are better placed than anyone to know what nonsense it all is!'

The others shot venomous glances at the speaker, at once envying the oblique flattery of her words and wondering how they might outdo her.

Dillon, another man rumoured to be the Queen's secret lover, entered the hall. Much was said of him, and widely believed. He confirmed nothing, denied nothing, and rejoiced in the persistent rumours. After all, what did it matter if it was untrue? The suspicion alone would greatly increase his standing among the women of the court.

It was Baron Besenval, however, who had amassed the largest audience of all. He was a big, broad-shouldered man, and though no longer young, he remained an imposing figure. He was also proving altogether less reticent.

'Now, I know for a fact that she has a secret chamber. Just a little room, simply furnished, but with…well, with all the necessaries!' He gave a quiet chuckle, and the lines around his eyes crinkled like the skin of an old apple. 'How would I know? Well, how do you think—I've been there myself! It's at the end of a dark corridor, past two garderobes. Where? Well, that would be telling, wouldn't it! But it's here in the palace. Tolerably comfortable, I should say, and of course it's also furnished with a bed! Oh yes, indeed!'

Well, this was just the sort of juicy gossip the court had been waiting for. They loathed the Queen, with that special loathing only envy can breed, and this made their outrage at her apparent hypocrisy taste all the sweeter.

'I can't say I'm surprised at her wanting a little place of that sort,' Besenval went on with a smirk. 'But I am a little surprised she had the nerve!'

He too had, for some time now, detested Marie-Antoinette. Ever since she invited him to that little room to ask him for help in preventing her brother-in-law from fighting a duel. Misreading the situation, he had propositioned her, and had been promptly ejected. Thus the words he spoke were quite true, while the implication behind them was pure slander.

This was his revenge.

'They'll be talking of this for a long time,' he thought, smiling with relish at the success of his gambit.

In addition to the three suspected lovers of the Queen, the most popular guest was a short, bespectacled, rather elderly gentleman. He was dressed in black, like an *abbé*, but wore white stockings. His name was Benjamin Franklin and he was the ambassador of the new American Republic. Rumour had it that he had already obtained an alliance from the King. A fleet was to be assembled and troops dispatched. Lafayette, they said, was already in Philadelphia. How exciting!

He was surrounded, in particular, by a throng of court ladies, who admired him rather in the manner of a rare and exotic beast. All were enthralled at the idea of liberty for the people. *Liberté*, the word was presently in vogue at court, and all were anxious to declare their support for it, and for the people. *Égalité*! *République*! How lovely! And peasants—what a wonderful, upright lot they were! The ladies naturally imagined peasants in the manner of Rousseau: gentle, wholesome folk who led their docile lambs to market on velvet halters and were forever dancing to tunes played on a shepherd's flute. And war! They pictured it rather like an extravagant carnival ball, full of dashing gallants in bright uniforms. A little danger, perhaps, but that only made the hero's kiss taste sweeter, and thick cannon smoke made as good a hiding place as any curtained alcove...

The handle turned, and the door opened.

Marie-Antoinette stepped inside.

Fersen bowed low, and when he straightened himself the Queen was already standing before the fireplace. Her face was in shadow and the faint candlelight illuminated only her bare neck and shoulders. Smooth skin, which gleamed like white porcelain or polished Carrara marble. An improbable pallor. So pale, indeed, that it took an effort to believe that this could truly be the body of a living, breathing woman, and not a statue made animate.

Perhaps she had deliberately chosen to stand with her back to the light, to conceal her face, but even so he could see that beneath her powder, the colour had drained from her cheeks.

'I have something very important to say, but only a little time... That is why I summoned you.'

She was in full court dress. Her hair rose in a high tower, decorated here and there with flowers and strings of diamonds. A circlet of diamonds surrounded a single egret feather. Her dress was of silver and gold, a wide, stiff crinoline from which hung cascades of pearls. The broad, hooped skirt made her appear more inaccessible than ever.

At her throat was a single jewel: the famous blue diamond, which was already said to be the cause of a thousand deaths, and to bear a thousand curses.

Fersen could not speak. He felt the approach of some fateful moment, and bowed again.

'You must leave the court,' the Queen said, then hesitated before continuing. 'That is what I summoned you here to say.'

Now at last, though he felt a cold hand clutch at his heart, Fersen found the words to speak.

'Why do you command me thus, Your Majesty?'

'Because you must. Do you understand? You must!'

'What has happened? Have I offended? Did I trespass? If so…'

'No. Not that.' The Queen paused again, and when she at last spoke it was as though her words came from some secret, locked place deep within her. 'Until now…until now I have survived on the general indifference of the court. On their apathy and disregard. Until now… Please, there is nothing more I can say, and nothing I can give you. Just, please… Please go!'

The young man fell to his knees before the Queen. He

understood now that this was a confession. That she loved him, and that these few, equivocal words were as much as she could say. A great wave of emotion, a confused mixture of sorrow and joy, coursed through him, and he bowed his head before this woman whom he adored. It was all he could do to hold back his tears.

Both were silent for a time, each conscious of their great, shared love.

At length, still kneeling and without looking up, Fersen spoke.

'Where should I go?'

The Queen's hand now strayed to the top of his head, and she lightly stroked his hair.

'I have given the matter much thought. The King is sending regiments to aid the Americans, and it would please me very much if you were to be among them. I should like to imagine you as a modern knight errant, venturing to far-off lands and doing battle for the sake of an ideal: the freedom of mankind.'

Raising his head, he met her gaze.

'I will go.'

A quiet knock sounded on the inner door, signalling that the royal procession was ready.

'I must leave now,' she whispered, and her slender forefinger traced a protective cross upon the forehead of the man kneeling before her. Then she held out her hand.

Fersen kissed it as holy relics are kissed, and as she at last withdrew it, two tears ran down his cheeks, then fell upon the place where his lips had been.

Before disappearing through the doorway, the Queen turned back one last time.

'God protect you!'

In the Hall of Mirrors, the twin doors to the royal apartments swung open. The first to emerge were the royal pages, dressed in robes of crimson velvet. They hurried through the hall, clearing a path for the procession. A crowd of onlookers quickly formed to either side of this route. The princesses and duchesses, who alone had the right to sit down at court and who in consequence had not risen from their chairs all evening, now pushed their way to the front. The master of ceremonies stepped forward, then rapped his staff three times upon the floor. All eyes now turned to the open doorway, as though waiting for the sun to rise on a new day.

At last the royal couple stepped into the hall, hand in hand. The King smiled benevolently upon the crowd, waving to left and right as he made his way through the hall. His slightly waddling gait caused him to bear his belly before him. The Queen walked by his side, head held high, gaze fixed directly in front of her. Perhaps she feared that, should her concentration lapse for an instant, the tears welling behind her lashes might begin to course down her cheeks.

Seeing her tremendous tower of hair, the young Duc de Lauzun gave an almost genuine exclamation of surprise.

'Oh joy! The Queen is wearing my egret feather in her hair!'

He was at once surrounded by inquisitive bystanders.

'Your what?'

'Your egret feather?'

'In her hair?'

Lauzun pretended he had not meant to speak out loud.

'Oh, goodness, it's nothing! I was wearing the feather, and the Queen mentioned that she liked it, so I gave it to her. But of course you mustn't think anything of it!'

'Oh, no, of course not! *Honi soit qui mal y pense!*'

They laughed, and friends nodded towards the duke, who had at once become as puffed up as a courting pigeon.

'She liked it, did she? Oh, I bet she liked it!'

This was met with a chorus of stifled giggles.

The royal couple passed slowly between the two throngs of courtiers, and the very same people who, just a moment before, had so greedily drunk in all that bile, slander and vitriol, and who had so gleefully done their part in spreading it, now bowed to the Queen with all outward signs of reverence and veneration.

The procession was close to the middle of the hall when

a portly gentleman entered through a small doorway at the rear of the gallery. He too was dressed in black, with satin knee breeches and black silk stockings. Only the cascades of lace which erupted from his waistcoat were white. And his cardinal's hat, perched upon his short clerical wig, was of course bright red. His name was Louis-René-Édouard de Rohan, the Prince-Bishop of Strasbourg.

Once inside, he crept towards a nearby pillar with the most conspicuous pretence at stealth which could be imagined. The greatest actor in the country could not have done better. He was, naturally, spotted at once, and a space was made for him—after all, he was one of the foremost churchmen in all of France.

The cardinal, however, demurred.

'No, no, thank you. I shall stay back here. You all know, after all, that I am out of favour. Publicly, at least!' He craned his neck, so as to see the royal couple. 'Ah, how lovely she looks! And her eyes are just as bright as they were earlier!'

He was judicious enough to break off his monologue there, for he had already said enough to spark rumours that he had been with the Queen not long before.

Sure enough, even before Marie-Antoinette's graceful form had glided out of earshot, everyone fell at once to eager gossip.

'So it's De Rohan who is the Queen's favourite? But then I suppose that's only natural: remember that it was he who brought her from Vienna in the first place. Perhaps that's when it all began!'

The crowd's estimation of the Prince-Bishop, who now stood discreetly against the far wall, rose considerably.

Fersen never knew how he reached the main staircase. It was deserted now—even the guard of honour had retired.

Stumbling like a sleepwalker, he slowly descended the stairs. At each step it seemed as though some part of his life was snapping. He felt faint and light-headed, and steadied himself by placing a hand on the marble balustrade. Once or twice he paused and leaned over that precipitous drop. Did it cross his mind to lean out a little further and simply tip himself over the edge?

Below him was a lively crowd of footmen. They knew that the ball would go on for many hours yet, so some stretched themselves out on the floor to get some rest, while others sauntered up and down, talking loudly. One or two young women had crept in, and occasionally let out little shrieks. It was strange to see these people, silent and rigid as automatons in the presence of their masters, now at liberty to express their true natures. They sprawled across chairs, bickered loudly among themselves, and pulled the girls into rough embraces.

How peculiar it was to peer down on all this from above. Fersen was only half conscious of it at the time. It was only days later that particular words and phrases, snagged like sheep's wool on the thorns of memory, came again to mind. And only much, much later did he piece together what he had heard, gazing down upon them like a bird in flight.

In the middle of the wide atrium stood a group of liveried footmen. They were reading passages from a pamphlet which one man held half hidden beneath his coat, and at almost every line they let out loud guffaws, half amused and half appalled by the author's effrontery.

'She's the crowned whore,' the man who held the book read aloud. 'And the best thing to do would be to strangle her in her bed—that's more or less the gist.'

A harsh, brutal voice, louder than the others, broke in.

'All of them! They should all be wiped out! They grow fat on the blood and sweat of the people! It's a fact—everything belongs to the people, and they are nothing but thieves! That's right, thieves!'

The speaker, a slovenly, frog-faced man, stepped towards these footmen in their bright liveries, scowling at them.

'And it's coming!' he said. 'We'll wipe them out yet! Kill them! Yes, we must kill them all, and then we shall have freedom!'

Fersen still peered over the edge of the balustrade, as though looking down into a well. All at once he had the impression that he had been cast down from heaven, and was now gazing deep into the pit of hell.

His eyes fell upon that black-haired, toad-like figure, and at the same instant the man saw him. He raised a hand, and to Fersen it seemed that he was shaking his fist towards him. Others clearly saw him too, however, for as if by magic, everyone at once stiffened and fell silent. Only the man with the grim, pock-marked face did not look away, but held his gaze with burning eyes.

Fersen descended the stairs and one of his footman hurried off to summon his carriage. He waited for it outside the main entrance, and a guard who recognised him saluted. Fersen smiled wanly, nodding towards the hall behind him.

'Are they always such a riot?'

'Yes, My Lord. They'll carry on like that all night, My Lord.'

Fersen gave an involuntary shudder. His next question was spoken almost mechanically.

'Who was that man in the black suit, the one who kept shouting?'

'Him? Oh, he's a mad one, My Lord,' the guardsman said. 'A doctor in the Duke of Artois' regiment of horse, I think. A real crackpot—totally off his rocker. What's his name again? Something like…Marat, I think.'

But Fersen, lost in his own thoughts, was no longer listening.

The carriage arrived and he climbed in. The two footmen leapt onto the backboard and the carriage jerked forward, bearing him off. Away from this overripe world of sweetness and decay, and towards a new world. Towards a world of battle, of warfare, and his first struggle for the freedom of mankind. The galloping horses carried him away, at the Queen's command. Fersen, the only man for whom her heart had ever learned to beat...

LEMEMAME

Foreword

We have decided that my old writing desk, after standing for so many years in a corner of the living room, should at long last be moved into one of the guest bedrooms.

'Very well then,' the reader may shrug, 'take a firm hold of both ends and heave! The thing is as good as done.'

Not so, alas, for before this particular desk can move so much as an inch it must be divested of all its many encrustations: there are great stacks of letters, notes, scribbled quotations, obituary notices, invitations and newspaper cuttings, all sifted and settled according to their age, like bands of sediment formed on a riverbed across eons of geological time. And that is before we even come to the drawers, each stuffed to bursting with drafts, doodles, sketches and Lord knows what else, slumbering in darkness across long years and decades.

Simply throwing it all away, however, does not bear thinking about. Buried in that heap, after all, could be a few old letters or scraps of information which, though useless for any other purpose, are still precious to me for the memories they contain. Though my chaotic approach to archiving means that finding any one particular thing is next to impossible, the advantage of this system—or rather, this absence of any system—is that everything is at least potentially to hand, and nothing is ever quite gone for good. What is needed is to go through it all and sort the whole lot out.

Easier said than done! One of the characteristics of old bits of paper is that they generate an inordinate amount of dust; five minutes spent leafing through old documents invariably leaves me coughing and spluttering, while my hands are no cleaner than if I had swept a chimney.

I begin to feel sorry for myself. Still, steeling my resolve, I tell myself that these hands can hardly get any dirtier now, and I might as well press on.

So I do.

A little later I have amassed a great heap of wastepaper on the floor beside me, and just eight or ten letters that seem worth holding on to. Then, from the depths of one of the drawers, a loosely tied bundle catches my eye. It falls apart, of course, as soon as I lift it.

Here are all the notes I wrote during that other world war, as well as my army travel pass from when, after a period of illness, I went to rejoin the Süd-Armee at Munkács[2] in 1915. There is also, wedged in between a few of my doodled caricatures, a field service map covering a section of the Carpathians, along with my army driving license and, in another envelope, the drafts of one or two reports which I wrote to István Tisza[3]. My section, I should explain, had been given certain confidential political commissions in addition to our military duties, and Tisza had ordered me to ensure that the rights of the local Ukrainian population were protected.

Digging deeper into this trove, I find more, including the little story which follows. I did not write it in Munkács, but later, after we had retaken Lemberg[4], so it must have been during the months after the Gorlice-Tarnów Offensive. During our eastward advance there was a battle at Stryi—a tough, ugly affair—and I spent three days in the trenches with the 21st Hungarian Honvéd battalion and the Prussian Guards Fusilier regiment, the so-called *Maikäfers*.

It was under the influence of what I saw there that I wrote this story, and I present it more or less intact, though as usual I had to delouse, brush and iron it before deeming it fit to be seen in public.

Not that I think the annals of Hungarian literature would have been any the poorer had it remained forever suspended in the miniature limbo of my desk drawer, but the fact is, I rather pity the poor thing. It is a sketchy, truncated, incomplete little story, but I feel rather as a neglectful father might, after having habitually disregarded the slowest and ugliest of his many children, only to find him living years later in some wretched hovel. Such a father, filled—one hopes—with remorse and shame, would clutch his abandoned offspring to his breast, then clean him up and dress him in the finest clothes, all the while cursing his own parental ineptitude. So too do I feel a certain shamefaced obligation to tie a ribbon upon this little story and present it to the world.

Lememame

It was a fine, clear day in June, the sky a vault of purest blue. Only in the west, from behind the low line of hills, did a dark stain smudge the sky. It was neither cloud nor morning mist, but smoke. The retreating Russians had set fire to the Drohobych oil wells and the plumes of smoke rose almost vertically into the sky, like pleats in a theatre curtain. It was a calm, windless summer day.

To the north was a low, wooded ridge, and below it a hillside of bare clay running down into the valley. To the right was a little hillock cloaked in rye, and the land there looked rich and good; the rye stalks were higher than a man, with ears already turning golden. Almost harvest time.

Soldiers were moving through the rye. They were Red Cross stretcher-bearers from the 21st Kolozsvár Honvéd battalion, looking for the wounded.

This plump, tranquil little valley had that morning been witness to a vicious skirmish. The Russians had been dug in at the edge of the wood and the 21st advanced towards them through the rye in skirmish order while the Prussian Maikäfers attacked their left flank across the boggy water-meadow.

That was why stretcher-bearers were now looking for our men in the rye: anyone shot in that dense mass was as good as invisible until one was almost right on top of him.

The 'undertakers', as we generally referred to Red Cross medics, would first crouch beside any fallen man and see whether he was still alive. Orders were, for now, to leave the dead where they lay, and to focus on evacuating the wounded.

The next step was to find out from a wounded man where exactly he had been hit, and whether he could still walk. Some could walk unaided, others only with their arm about a companion's shoulder, and still others needed to be stretchered out. Whenever they found an unconscious man they would first check whether he was alive, then call out to a comrade elsewhere in the field to bring up the stretcher.

The stretcher-bearers paced the field with slow, heavy steps, stopping often to talk. They were Romanians from the Transylvanian Mezőség, less enthusiastic soldiers than their Hungarian-speaking neighbours from the Kalotaszeg, or upland districts, and in any case little given to urgency at the best of times: even their haystacks back home were built very slowly, after much idle chat and consultation.

Still, it is unfair to generalise: there are plenty of quick, spry, energetic men among the Romanians, and perhaps the quickest of all was Lememame.

This was a nickname. His real name was Tudor Tiptiş, but everyone in his village of Mezőbányica[5] had always called him Lememame, a childish corruption of *laptemină*, or 'milkface.' This name had stuck because of his strikingly blonde features; the little moustache above his upper lip was so pale it could scarcely be seen, while his plump face was as pink as any newborn's. That is why everyone called him Lememame.

His section was at the far edge of the field, on the right flank of the little hillock, and the head-high rye parted before him as he pushed into it. It seemed even more thickly planted here than at the bottom of the hill, but he guessed it could only be about a hundred yards or so to the tree line.

Crows perched in the trees. Hooded crows. Magpies hopped from branch to branch.

Lememame knew what that meant: there were dead or dying men out there, and these carrion birds watched them with black, beady eyes. He pressed on about twenty or thirty paces through the rye, then stopped in sudden fright. Someone was lying at his feet, so well concealed beneath the crushed stalks that he almost stepped on him. At first he could only see leather boots and a pair of field-grey service trousers, but after pulling away the rye he saw the man's face.

And recognised him.

It was Sergeant Cioban, or Big Dumitru, as everyone called him. He was lying on his back, entirely motionless, but long, rasping gasps showed that he was still alive. His arms were splayed, and the back of his head seemed to be propped on some clod of dirt, for his chin was pressed down into his open collar.

Lememame at once knelt down next to him.

'So it's you is it?' he asked. 'Cioban?'

This was an unnecessary question—there was no mistaking the man's identity—but Lememame was not expecting an answer.

The wounded man tried to speak. The mouth under his big black moustache formed shapes and his tongue moved between two rows of white teeth, but no sound came. His whole body spasmed with the enormous effort, and veins stood out on his forehead, but still there were no words, just a long, pain-stricken moan. That muteness, however, only made his grey eyes—bloodshot and wide with terror—all the more expressive. They were searching Lememame's face for any sign of pity.

The two men were silent for a few moments, looking at one another, then Lememame spoke again, only to say the same words as before.

'So it's you is it? Cioban?'

In his voice there now sounded a note of scornful amusement, while the stricken man's only response was the same pitiable moan.

'And you can't speak, eh? Not a peep? And movement? Nothing doing there, either? How about we give it a try?'

Taking Cioban by the hand and elbow, he hauled him off the ground. Then let go. Cioban fell heavily backwards, as nerveless as a corpse.

'So it's like that is it? Barrel of laughs you are! What did you cop, then? Bullet to the spine? That'll be what it is, all right; you can take my word for it. Ugly bastard of a wound, too. Very ugly. It'll be deep inside you, that bullet. Can't speak either? No, don't keep straining yourself, it won't do any good!'

Lememame trampled down the rye stalks around Cioban then squatted down next to him, comfortably resting his weight on the balls of his feet, the way shepherds do.

'But you want to know something?' he whispered. 'I can speak, and I can still walk too! I can move, run, jump—and see this hand? I can move it anywhere I want, easy as that! Around your neck, for instance, if I feel like it.'

He was silent for another moment, then gave a quiet chuckle.

'Just think, what were the chances that I should be the one to find you? The very man you've been tormenting since I was a boy. Remember? You couldn't get enough of torturing me. And now here we are! Maybe your memory's hazy, you bastard, so I'll tell you how it was!'

Reflecting for a moment, he turned and spat into the rye before speaking.

'Remember? It was ten years ago, maybe more, and the good Lord had granted us a fine crop of plums; more plums than I had ever seen. I was still just a young lad then, and one evening I climbed up the priest's garden wall; the one at the far end, facing the road. Could anyone really have blamed me? I was just a poor wretch, and the priest had more plums than he knew what to do with! Then you came up the road and saw me. I saw you too, and knew you were a bad man. I jumped down and ran, but you were too fast; you caught me and beat me. Beat me bloody. Tell me, what were the priest's plums to you?'

He paused, as though expecting a response, then went on.

'Nothing! Nothing! Not a damned thing! You beat me for the fun of it! And not just with your fists, either, but with a post you broke off the fence! You broke my finger too, remember? This one! That's why I became a stretcher-bearer, because I still can't bend it properly. And it wasn't enough just to beat me senseless, was it? You had to steal my hat, too; the one I was carrying the plums in. You took the hat, took the plums, and strolled home chuckling to yourself, didn't you? That's what you did to me that day, Dumitru Cioban.'

The wounded man plainly wanted to speak, perhaps to defend his actions or else to beg forgiveness. His lips moved, but no words came. A thin trickle of blood ran from one corner of his mouth to his chin while Lememame watched impassively; only his eyes glinted beneath straw-coloured brows. He surveyed his enemy for a long time.

Two fat flies suddenly appeared, their abdomens an iridescent blue. Carrion flies. They buzzed about Cioban's face, landing on his cheeks and chin with as much stinging force as if they had been flung at him. They landed, then took off, then landed again, as though drunk on the taste of fresh blood. There was no sound at all besides the buzzing of these two flies; all else was silence. Then Lememame spoke.

'And what about Viorica?'

He pursed his lips, then repeated the name.

'Viorica.'

For a few moments he was silent, and in his mind's eye there appeared the image of a sweet, pretty girl. How pretty! Cheeks like two red apples and eyes that shone with the deep, lustrous brown of a freshly hulled chestnut. He had danced with her or before her, for her beauty, more times than he could count, for he was a great dancer. The best in the village. There was nobody who could dance the *căluş* like him, for it is an intricate dance and requires much skill.

At first the boys dance among themselves, weaving in and out with quick, tapping steps. Everyone wears garters strung with rattles and bells, tied loosely about the knees. This is why they have to move with such quick, jiggling steps, to prevent the garters slipping off. Only the deftest footwork can keep them up and a skilful performance is a marvel to behold; the bells ring loudest when the garter is free to move up and down the calf. Bells are also tied to the dancer's ankles, and to the toes of his shoes, and if he is a true master then he also carries a long stick which he spins in front of him or above his head. Sometimes he leaps high into the air and the stick appears for a miraculous instant beneath his upraised legs, then both heels come crashing down and the dance goes on as though nothing very extraordinary had happened.

The girls, meanwhile, whisper to one another behind their hands, and the spectators clap and cheer.

Nobody could dance like Lememame, and nobody's bells rang so loud and clear as his, perhaps because his strong, muscular calves allowed him to tie his garters more loosely than anyone else. He could hold himself aloft, balancing on the end of his stick, for longer than the others, and even sang rhymed verses as he danced. The effect was breathtaking, and the girls watching this handsome young dancer all blushed and giggled.

Viorica knew that after the boys' dance he would pick her as his partner. That was why she sat behind two or three rows of girls. She would not let him choose her from the front row, as if at random, but would make him seek her out and pull her forward. It was always like that: Lememame would reach across the heads of the other girls and seize her by the collar, then try to drag her to the front. She, of course, would shriek and squirm and try to get away, just as was expected of her, and only stop when the boy had succeeded in clasping her in an embrace. After that she would cling to him, dancing as meekly as a lamb.

The dances were wonderful, but still better were their Sunday-evening trysts. In early spring, when the grass had hardly begun to sprout and only the broom bushes were thick with leaves, they would walk together, down to the willow-fringed stream. Peewits called from the fringes of the marsh, the alders already echoed to the cuckoo's two-tone song, and towards dusk the nightingale gave a practice trill, though it was not yet dark enough for him to launch into his true song. That was the hour of the day when they would sit together in some shadowed spot, their conjoined fingers weaving a complex, ever-changing knot, their lips meeting in long kisses.

Sometimes it was long past dark by the time Viorica got home, and her father would beat her. Not much, but more for appearance's sake. This was no great hardship, and Viorica did not blame him; she knew that it was only natural, and her pitiful cries were likewise for show.

In summer, when the hay was being gathered, they sat together in the shade of a haystack, and at reaping time they strolled the labyrinth of ripe corn stocks.

That is how it was, and it was beautiful.

Perhaps with time he could have married Viorica, though she was the daughter of a prosperous farmer while he had nothing but a cotter's shack and a little garden. Still, he was a bright, industrious youth, good with his hands and rarely drunk. He was willing to lend a hand, too, and Viorica's father was glad of his help when it came to the heavy work which always needs doing around a farm. He helped cut down trees, weave a new wicker fence, re-tile the outhouse roof and even rig a new jib for the sweep-well. This was all done simply as a favour, of course, and he never asked for payment, but his assistance was much appreciated and at times her father expressly asked him to visit. So he came to spend a lot of time at Viorica's house, and often dropped by to ask if anything needed doing. If he happened to be on his way to the markets at Dedrád or Szászrégen he would ask if there was anything he could pick up for them, and he always brought back a kerchief, an almond pastry, a string of glass beads, or some other little present for Viorica. At such times nobody minded if Viorica slipped off through the corn with him, nor if she tarried in returning home.

That autumn, however, Cioban came back from the army. He had served for six years: three with the 21st and three as a sergeant in the gendarmes[6]. His means were barely any more substantial than Lememame's, but he received a veteran's pension, which is no trifle in a village like Mezőbányica. More than that, he was a strong, brutal man, with a big voice often raised in anger. He had a bristling moustache and big, heavy hands that could land savage punches: anyone struck by that right fist was laid out flat.

He soon became a figure of consequence in the district, and everyone feared him. When they saw him coming, they always greeted him respectfully. He also lived, as it happens, just two plots away from Viorica's house, and three days after his return she caught his eye.

He did not speak to her, but went to her father instead. He asked for her, and her father agreed. How could he not? He too feared Cioban, not merely on account of his voice and his fists, but also because he threatened to 'report' anyone who refused to do his bidding. His background in the gendarmes meant that he knew the law from top to bottom, and he was paid money by the state, which to these remote villagers was an alarming mystery suggesting powers beyond their ken.

Viorica shrieked and cried, fought and pleaded.

Lememame was at once forbidden to visit the house and from that day on, he was never allowed even to set foot upon their land. If they found him loitering nearby he was chased away, and from his neighbouring farm Cioban set his dogs upon the young man. If Viorica slipped out in the evening to meet him then her father or her older brother would catch and beat her, not for show as before, but viciously. Even at the dances Cioban shadowed her, and she was not allowed to share so much as a private word with Lememame. Nor did she try; it would only have meant another beating.

That is how it was.

Still, despite all this, he and Viorica held out for a long time. One afternoon she went to wash clothes in the stream, and Lememame followed her. He thought he was being careful; instead of going after her directly he went up into the woods, then slipped down behind the high riverbank and followed it to the washing place. He emerged before her from a high stand of riverside broom. Hardly had he reached her, though, hardly had they embraced, than the fearful figure of Cioban descended upon them, beating, punching and kicking Lememame so savagely that he had to be carried home. For two days and two nights he spat blood and could not leave his bed.

That is how it happened.

So Viorica married Sergeant Cioban. Lememame left the village and went into service in Szászrégen. He did so not from financial want but because he could not bear the pain of meeting Viorica in the street. Better never to see her again. He could not join the army on account of his crippled finger, so he moved to the county town. He lived there for three years, and if someone from Mezőbányica came to the weekly market, they often stopped to chat with him. At last, cautiously, the conversation would turn to Viorica. He could not help asking, though whatever he heard always caused him pain.

He heard that she was pregnant. That she had given birth to a little girl. That the poor thing did not survive, but died after three weeks. That her husband beat her much and often, and that her own health was bad. She was sick. She coughed. A doctor had been called from Teke, which was only done when things were very bad. At last he heard that poor Viorica had died.

That is how it was. The funeral had been a year earlier but he did not go. He would never go back.

Then had come the war, and mobilisation. He was called up as a reservist in the 21st Kolozsvárs. It was fortunate that he had been made a stretcher-bearer, since it meant he was not directly under Cioban's thumb. Had that been the case he might not have survived, but even as it was Cioban succeeded in making trouble for him with the other soldiers.

But now here he was! Powerless. And just the two of them. They were hidden in the rye, where nobody else would see them, as alone as if they were the last two left in all creation. No law and no recourse. Let the bastard pay!

'Viorica. You remember? You took her from me, tore us apart, though you knew perfectly well we were in love. Why? Because you like to hurt, don't you? You like to kill. I know that now. I know you killed her, and you know it too, don't you?'

Again he paused as though expecting an answer, then gave a long, merciless, sardonic laugh.

'Don't deny it, it's not worth the effort. You're the type that'll say anything. That's the way it is, but I know you killed her. *Dracul*! Devil!'

Cioban opened his mouth again, perhaps wider than before, and made his most desperate effort to speak. It was dreadful to watch as those wrenching, convulsive efforts resulted in nothing. His eyebrows rose in pleading arcs, his face contorted in an awful grimace, but from his throat came nothing but that low, drawn-out, almost animal howl, as a mixture of blood and saliva trickled once more from the corner of his mouth.

The iridescent flies returned, but now there were more of them, and they flew straight for the wounded man's face. They crawled across his nose and cheeks, seeking the warmer, more humid orifices of his mouth and eyes.

Lememame, however, took out his handkerchief and brushed them away, then wiped the blood from Cioban's chin; he did not want his enemy to think of anything besides his own words. Let the flies return later, after he had gone.

Then they were welcome to him, but no distractions now. All the same, he could make use of them.

'See? The carrion flies are already here; they'll share you with the worms. And you hear that chatter? Those are magpies. You can't see them, but I can. More importantly, they can see you, and there are big crows with them in the trees. Hear that? That was one of them cawing. They'll take your eyes, Cioban, one by one, and they won't even have to wait until you're dead. Why would they? You can't lift a finger! I'm going to leave you, see, just the way you are. This is where you'll rot, which is just what you deserve.'

Lememame rose. He stood straight, legs apart and chest out, as though sheer exultation had inflated not just his cheeks but his entire body. He made an imposing sight.

He said nothing for a few moments, savouring his enemy's utter helplessness. Then it was time to go.

'You know, I'd have forgiven that first beating in the plum orchard, and probably even that second one by the riverbank, but I can never forgive what you did to poor, sweet Viorica. I haven't forgotten the way you kept hounding me here too, for no reason, telling lies about me and having my captain punish me. I'm leaving now, but you'll stay right here. You'll stay right here in the rye, until *Dracul* himself comes and drags you down to hell. That's where you belong, Cioban.'

The stricken man, doubtless making one last, desperate attempt to plead for mercy, succeeded in bringing some sound to his lips. It was a thin, pitiable sound, the sort of short, broken yelps that tiny puppies make when still blind. Tears started in his wide-open eyes. This made no impression on Lememame, who just laughed.

'You squeal like a suckling pig, Cioban, but you've only yourself to blame!'

He set off, but turned back after a couple of steps. Taking off his cap, he clicked his heels and gave a crisp military salute.

'Sergeant Cioban! Good luck, sergeant!'

Then with slow, plodding steps he set off through the rye towards the hilltop, sweeping back and forth just as he had before. Now and again he stopped and looked around, then set off again. He paused ever more frequently, perhaps hesitating, or perhaps because the hillside was steep here. He was already close to the summit when he stopped again and looked back.

Further down a magpie had already flown past him, so low that its wing tips almost skimmed the ears of rye, before alighting on a hawthorn bush at the edge of the wood. Its flight must have taken it right over the prone, helpless body of Cioban. The magpie gave a raucous squawk, then took off again, flying right over the place where Cioban lay.

One or two crows cawed.

Lememame stood for a long time near the crest of that little hill, watching the birds. Now another magpie took off, and he watched that one too as it flew over the same spot. It was also taking a look, and landed in the same hawthorn bush. Then it gave the same squawk, hopping up and down the branch as though to signal that it had found food.

More crows cawed.

Lememame shook his head, stamped down hard with one foot, then set off again. On the crest of the hill he stopped, panting for breath.

Most of his Red Cross comrades had moved a good distance away while he had been on the far side. They had brought out everyone they had found in the rye, and were now searching the adjacent cornfield. There were only one or two still at the far end of the rye field, up by the trees, and they were making their way towards the dressing station.

Lememame just stood with lowered head, as though pondering something. That was when his comrade, a young Hungarian from Bikal[7], called out to him from the tree line.

'Oi! You! Did you find any wounded?'

Lememame did not respond, and the man had to repeat his question twice.

'Did you find anyone?' He then added, 'If not then come on! We're moving out!'

Lememame still hesitated, puffing his cheeks as though catching his breath. Then at last he answered.

'I did. Bring up the stretcher...'

THE EMPEROR'S SECRET

Urkan, crimson-browed lord of the sky, sank towards the horizon. He was heading westward, across the *limes*, the frontiers of the Roman Empire, towards the imperial heartlands of Italy and Gaul, and his fiery glance fell upon all the lands ravaged and despoiled by the Huns. As he neared the low hills marking the edge of the plains he seemed to slow, as though tempted to linger a moment above the glittering waters of the Danube. Then at once he was gone, disappearing as warriors do when laying an ambush, leaving nothing but a red stain at the foot of the sky. Even the scraps of cloud along the horizon burned like distant villages.

Night fell on the great plains, as quickly and inexorably as a rising flood.

A guard stood by the rim of the pit, his upper body still catching the last light of day but his legs below the knee already in shadow. He was leaning on a long spear, easy and motionless as a shepherd, looking towards the west. Towards Roman Pannonia. Towards Rome. He was of the Qangli people, who served the Huns as carters. This stocky little man was standing guard, for this pit was a prison, and held an important prisoner.

Wherever the Huns made their camp and the womenfolk erected shelters, there, some distance from their living quarters, a deep and spacious hole was dug. This was the nomads' prison, and held any captives they judged worth the trouble of keeping.

This prisoner was valuable because he had once been a great man, the envoy of an emperor. Not the emperor of the Romans but the Son of Heaven, ruler of the Middle Kingdom. Hun raiders had captured him far, far to the east, beyond even the lands of Khwarazm, on the farthest reaches of the Persian Empire. They had been pillaging the rich northern oases of the Sasanians, just as they were now pillaging the lands of the Romans. That had been many years before.

An imperial Chinese embassy had embarked on the long journey home from the Persian capital of Ctesiphon, laden with gifts and rich treasures from the Shah, and escorted by two hundred Persian bodyguards hand-picked for their menacing scowls and bristling moustaches. The richest treasure of all, however, was in the personal possession of the mandarin envoy himself, Kung, ambassador of the Son of Heaven. He alone had brought to Persia the message whispered in his ear by the celestial sovereign of the Middle Kingdom and he alone carried within his breast the Shah's reply: the offer of an alliance.

But the caravan was attacked by Hun horsemen, and those scowling, moustachioed bodyguards all fled. The whole embassy was enslaved, and the gold and silver was distributed among the followers of the Hun warlord. The only treasure they did not steal was the one in Kung's breast: the Emperor's secret. Since then, Kung had lived in a series of Hun prison pits, always about four or five arrowshots from the main camp. For many years.

He spent his days sitting at the bottom of his pit, looking up at the sky. If it snowed, the pit filled up with snow, and if it rained, it filled with rain. Filthy, cloudy water that turned the dirt floor to mud. Somehow, the musty scent of clay always brought to mind the perfumed baths of his home in Jianye.

Now too he was looking up at the sky. His bald head tilted back, legs crossed and arms folded across his chest above the golden dragon. The Magnificent and Terrible High Lord of all the Huns had permitted him—perhaps in mockery —to keep his formal ambassadorial robes. They were of aquamarine silk, with two golden dragons embroidered on the front and back, and rising tongues of golden flame. The silk had long since rotted, of course, but the embroidery still clung to him like a tattered web. Despite the passage of years and the accumulation of filth, those snarling dragons still flared their nostrils and pawed the air with their four-clawed feet, as menacingly as when they first bestrode that silken ground. Now there was no background at all besides the naked body of Kung himself, so that one might have taken those beasts for demons, sent to bite and tear the old man's emaciated flesh.

Kung gazed continually at the sun, watching as it made the same journey from the east that he had made all those years before. His tiny, half-blinded eyes followed its progress, as though stubbornly, hopelessly hoping that just once it might slow, then stop, then set off back the way it had come. Back east.

Back home.

Even when the sun had disappeared below the horizon, still the old prisoner continued to look. He did not simply stare blankly into the darkness, but looked, as though examining a distant object. As though he saw something. At such times his eyes often opened wide, blinking rapidly, and his face would contort into a horrifying rictus of fear.

Perhaps he was thinking back to the great tortures he had endured, when the ancient, well-worn methods were twice tried upon him, to make him divulge the Emperor's secret. One by one they had torn out his fingernails, and bent back three fingers of his right hand until they snapped. Twice they had furrowed his skin with red-hot irons, from one end to the other. They had employed all their wickedness and all their cunning in a succession of gradually escalating torments, but though they crippled him, he never said a word.

The Emperor's secret was a secret still.

'You'll stay in this pit until you talk!' the Magnificent and Terrible High Lord of all the Huns had said.

That had been long ago.

Or was he perhaps tormented by doubt, pondering the outcome of his mission? Had the combined forces of the Persians and the Chinese defeated the Hun horde? Had they come to this strange Western land because they were checked and bloodied in the East, or because they had run out of foes to conquer? He had heard nothing of any Persian campaign, nor could he ask anyone without risking some inadvertent betrayal of his secret. Nor could he even overhear anything, since his guards were always from the Qangli or Tunguz, tribes considered menial by the Huns, and kept ignorant of the great matters of the world. A long white beard now grew from his chin, with thinner strands tufting his cheeks and a great moustache falling across his mouth, but in all those long years, Kung never heard the merest scrap of news about the cause for which he had been martyred. Here he lived, buried alive in a hole in the ground.

Night fell. The black sky was speckled with countless points of light: the tiny windows through which Tammus, boar-goddess of the Hun pantheon, peers down upon the terrestrial world.

The Qangli guard looked down at the prisoner.

'Get up, old man! Let's go!'

It took him a few minutes to get to his feet. Hardly a surprise: he truly was an old man, and besides his crippled right hand he was also chained to a long iron bar. This was to prevent him running, were he somehow to escape his pit. He moaned, and his chest heaved from the exertion, but he climbed out on his own.

The Qangli, a good-natured boy, waited until the prisoner had got his breath back. Then he spoke again.

'Let's go, old man!'

He lifted the prisoner's iron so it would not drag along the ground, then set off towards a distant camp-fire where some men had gathered to eat and talk. They did this most nights, after the overseer responsible for the captives had gone to bed. They walked through the darkness, tonight as every night: the friendly young Qangli in front, carrying a spear in his right hand and the bar of iron in the other, and followed obediently by the envoy of the Son of Heaven.

They went slowly, and the camp-fire was far away. It took them an hour and a half to reach it. Arriving at last, they sat down in a circle close to the flames, on the same coarse rugs and capes as usual.

Their host, a Massagetean farmer, was a tall, broad-shouldered, red-haired man, his well-fed body tanned to the golden brown of baked bread, and he greeted his guests in congenial, Slavic fashion. He was especially solicitous towards the Chinese envoy, knowing—as everybody did—that he had twice been given 'the irons' and never talked.

No small thing.

The old man was, accordingly, given the place of honour by the fire, to the left of the host: the 'heart side.' The Massagetean sat everyone by order of precedence. To his right were the two Tunguz herders. They also were bondsmen, but they worked on horseback and that in itself compelled respect. Their dark, slightly scornful Turanian faces showed that they expected no less. They ate little, spoke little, and their eyes only gleamed if there was talk of battle. Next came a shepherd, the son of the Massagetean farmer, and opposite him the Qangli. Everyone in his right place. The dogs too had their order of precedence: the sheepdogs guarded their spot by the fire, where they were given boiled horseflesh to eat, and did not allow the camp dogs to pass beyond the wicker windbreak. This too was proper. The only difference between the job of the shepherd and the sheepdog was that the sheepdog did not have to carry water jars.

Tonight there was one more guest in the circle, a late arrival who had only appeared at sundown. He too was an Easterner, a Gepid, with a long beard and somewhat Teutonic features. His hair was tied a knot above his forehead. The newcomer sat farthest from the host, for while the Massagetean was a convivial man, he was also prudent. Let this stranger sit by the two Tunguz; nobody made trouble with them.

Conversation proceeded quietly, with long pauses. All spoke Hunnic, for though none of them was a true Hun, it was the only language everyone understood.

Curious who the stranger might be, Kung cautiously and courteously asked where he was from.

'Far away,' said the Gepid. 'Far away.' With a broad, vague movement of the arm he gestured towards the east.

'From the mountains?'

'Beyond the mountains. Beyond the great plain. Beyond the Atil river.' Again he gestured expansively towards the east.

Kung's eyes shone, and only long and excellent training held his placid expression in place. Nothing in his voice betrayed how unspeakably important the next question was:

'Much fighting out there?'

The Gepid shrugged. 'No end of fighting.'

Deciding to elaborate, he told a long and convoluted story of how a Gepid tribe had done battle with some unknown people over a stolen idol. The Massageteans listened with interest, the Tunguz smiled disdainfully, and Kung gave not the slightest indication of how bored he was. He listened attentively to the very end, and only when the stranger had finished did he ask another question.

'There were no other wars out there? No great battle between armies of thousands? I mean, for instance… between the Huns and some other great power? Long ago?'

The Gepid's blue eyes looked at him, nonplussed. He

was clearly trying to remember, but could think of nothing that matched the old man's description. Reaching up, his fingers played with the knot of hair on his head, as though searching it for a forgotten memory.

'Hun armies? No, I don't remember anything like that.'

So he too knew nothing. Nothing about the Khwarazmian campaign and the alliance between the Persian Shah and the Emperor of China. Nothing. The uncertainty was wretched.

The shepherd brought food. He was an insolent young man, and being the son of the Massagetean farmer he felt free to do as he pleased. There was almost no gap between his mouth and his turned-up nose, and when seen from below in the firelight it was easy to believe he had begun life as a squealing piglet, made human only by some deity's mistake or cheerful caprice. Every night he sneered at old Kung and made the same oafish joke.

'Put in a good shift, did you? There's no food for those that don't pull their weight.'

The Tunguz gave their usual scornful smile. They did little enough work themselves. Kung gave the same answer, word for word, as he had given the night before, and all the nights before that for longer than he could remember.

'Useful work is its own reward. They are blind who judge the value of work only by what it pays. Thus the wise man says: use your reason, and cultivate the seeds of knowing and doing in your soul.'

He knew they would laugh; none understood, the young shepherd least of all. He said it for himself, because it was good to hear, even on his own lips, some faint breath of civilisation. He could imagine himself for a moment in the halls of Chang An, among mandarins and scholars. He strove, even here, to preserve in every particular the habits and deportment of a Chinese gentleman, as though he really were in the finest Imperial society. He ate his boiled horseflesh with dignity and refinement, though impeded somewhat by his three crippled fingers, and if a question was asked of him he answered it fully, with measured politeness. In this he never wavered, though they asked him many stupid and cruel questions. They took him for a great liar, and made him talk to listen to his lies. With winks and chuckles they asked him if he had ever been a rich man, and if he had a family.

The Chinese envoy answered with the same careful words as every night. He told them he had once been a great lord in his own land, and a favourite of the Emperor. The great Emperor, the Son of Heaven, who lived in a golden palace. He often lingered in his descriptions of that gorgeous palace, and of the Emperor too, for though he was young he had wisdom, and was a good man. The old man told them of his home in Jianye, of the peonies that grew in his flower garden and his collection of rare porcelains. He talked about his daughter—his one, heartbreakingly lovely daughter— betrothed to a handsome young prince.

The barbarians laughed at this most of all, and the pig-faced young man interrupted.

'I'll bet the slavers have long since sold off your pretty daughter, and all your pretty grandchildren too!'

His coarseness provoked uproarious laughter; the Massagetean farmer put both hands on his drum-like belly as though afraid it would roll away from too much mirth. The Gepid rocked back and forth, his laughter high and birdlike, and even the two Tunguz grinned and slapped their thighs.

'I'll bet! I'll just bet they have!'

Kung waited patiently until the laughter subsided, then went on. Not a muscle of his face twitched, and though they continually baited and insulted him, he remained always a model of polite composure.

To celebrate the betrothal he had given a great dowry, one befitting a prince, as well as a very old painting and many masterpieces of metalwork and enamelling. He told them what the painting depicted, and the fine words running down its right-hand border. It was the privilege of the cultivated soul, it said, to lose oneself in the contemplation of art's divine mystery, which captured for all eternity the feather-light, ungraspable loveliness of a fleeting moment. He had given it because it was his daughter's favourite.

So spoke Kung, envoy of the Son of Heaven. He talked about everything in great detail, and only one thing never passed his lips: the Emperor's secret. That great treasure was buried deep within his soul.

Somewhere out in the darkness a dog barked. The other dogs pricked their ears, and soon they were all barking.

The Massageteans leapt to their feet. Who was out there? The Tunguz reached for their bows and the Gepid hefted his axe. The pig-faced lad went out beyond the wicker windbreak, but hurried back almost immediately. His face was pale.

'Huns. On horseback.'

They craned their necks and saw the black silhouettes of horsemen against the treeless horizon. Those high saddles and wickedly long, double-recurve bows... Even in silhouette there was something uniquely dreadful about a mounted Hun. The shepherds hissed to their dogs to come close: woe to him whose dog spooked a Hun lord's horse!

As the horsemen approached, the Massageteans, the Gepid, the Qangli guard and even the scornful Tunguz knelt before them in the dirt.

Only Kung remained motionless by the fire.

The horsemen trotted through the opening in the wicker fence, then dismounted and stepped on the prostrate men before them. The fat Massagetean began to introduce himself.

'Your unworthy servant Draguts, head farmer to the priests of Urkan. Welcome, noble lords, in the name of the high gods!'

The leading Hun was still on horseback. He must have been a very great lord, a leader of many men, for the saddle blanket of his horse was sequinned with a hundred silver shards.

'Water. Where's the spring?' he asked.

Without lifting his head from the dirt, the old shepherd extended a hand.

'That way, My Lord, not a hundred paces.'

The cowering farmer crept forward to hold the bridle of the Hun's horse, while the Qangli guard knelt by his stirrup with his forehead in the dust to act as a step for the warrior to dismount.

'Water the horses. Then we ride on.'

The two most distinguished Huns handed their horses' reins to a younger companion, who led them towards the spring. Both high-ranking men were short and stocky, with broad shoulders. They wore high-pointed, black felt caps, and the faces beneath them seemed uncommonly dark. Their moleskin mantles, long and shapeless as caftans, had a velvety softness entirely at odds with those hard features. Only their bright silk belts showed any colour.

Kung sat by the fire, motionless as a carved idol. His legs were folded under him, his hands palm-down on his knees, and in the firelight the dragons round his chest shimmered and stirred. They were a part of him now, stitched into his very skin or breaking out from within his ruined body. So still was he that, had it not been for his long, feathery beard twitching in rhythmic unison with his breath, he would hardly have seemed alive at all.

'Who is the old man?' demanded the lead Hun.

The others, most of whom had quietly fled beyond the wicker fence, exchanged terrified glances. In their alarm at the Huns' arrival they had completely forgotten about Kung. What would happen now? The poor Qangli guard almost fainted with fright.

The leading Hun spoke again, his voice more peremptory than ever.

'Who are you?'

'I am a servant of the Emperor of China,' Kung said quietly. 'And who, young man, are you?'

The Massagetean farmer, his last scrap of courage gone, crept away towards the fire. He went backwards, bobbing his head and babbling a stream of flattery and self-abnegation. He also told the Hun everything the old Chinese man had said about himself, not because he believed a word of it, but because he hoped that ceaseless talking might blunt the Hun's anger at the old prisoner's insolence.

'Enough!'

The two Huns crouched by the fire. They had taken an interest in the old man: his lordly manner intrigued them, and if he had truly endured the great tortures twice and held his tongue, then that was an impressive feat.

They began to speak with him, observing that Eastern convention whereby parsimonious speech is considered a mark of politeness, and asked him why and for how long he had been among the Huns.

Kung answered politely and dispassionately, giving nothing but the essential facts. What he told them was, he thought, only those things that everyone knew. What the whole world knew. That he had been captured on Persian territory long ago, and that the Huns had used every technique of torture to force him to divulge his secret. The secret entrusted to him. He had said nothing, and had been a prisoner ever since.

Neither his expression nor his tone of voice altered in the slightest as he told his tale, and pride only fleetingly glinted in his eye when he told of the great tortures he had endured, all without giving up his great secret. Still they did not know! That was the thought behind the glint in his eye: the Emperor's secret was a secret still.

At length the old man finished, and there was a moment's silence round the camp-fire. Then he spoke again.

'Perhaps, young warrior, that is the reason you have come? To take me again to the torture bench? Perhaps the Magnificent and Terrible Lord of all the Huns has grown tired of waiting for me to speak. Well, I am ready. Further interrogation is a matter of indifference to me: he who serves an immortal cause possesses immortal will. Thus the wise man says: Nothing occupies my spirit which is not of the utmost importance.' Politely, with a grave and confident smile, he looked at the two warriors. 'I must regrettably inform you that I shall be able to divulge no more than on the previous two occasions.'

The Hun chief did not reply, but just gazed into the depths of the fire. Flickering embers danced, reflected in eyes that were as sharp and grey as an eagle-owl's. After a pause he asked again how long the old man had been a prisoner.

'Thirty years,' answered Kung.

The Hun then asked if there was anything about which the old man might be curious.

'There is,' answered the Emperor's envoy. 'And if you do me this service I will—for it is all I can do—hold you forever in grateful memory. All I wish for is some information about events long past, and for you to answer as truthfully as you can. Tell me, were armies ever led east, and if so, what befell them?'

'To the east? A war? Not to my knowledge. I don't remember the Magnificent and Terrible Lord sending armies into the lands east of here. Last winter there was a great war to the west, though; we crushed the Franks and pursued them across the Rhine. Would you like to hear that story?'

'No,' Kung smiled thinly. 'To the east. I know for a fact that there was a great war there around thirty years ago. Please, try to remember.'

He hesitated, afraid that to say more might betray some part of his secret. Then he spoke again.

'Against the Empire of the Persians.'

Now the other Hun, a few years older than his companion, spoke.

'The old man is right. I heard from my father that a great army was led against the Persians. Our tribe was in the vanguard, I know that.'

'Well? And? What happened?' Kung eagerly extended his thin neck. 'Please, tell me. Tell me what happened.'

'I know no more than that; only that there was some hard fighting.'

'Yes,' said the other. 'There was fighting out there in those days, I remember hearing about it too.' He thought for a few minutes, then frowned and shook his head. 'There was fighting out there, but I don't know what came of it. That was a long time ago, old man. Who cares?'

Kung's face fell. So nobody knew? Not even these men, privy to all the high councils of the Huns?

The chief Hun exchanged a few whispered words with his companion, then turned to scowl at the men beyond the fence.

'Where is this prisoner's guard? Bring him before us.'

Half dead with fright, the ashen-faced Qangli was hauled into the firelight. The Massagetean, the two Tunguz and even the Gepid newcomer officiously dragged him out of the shadows, tossing him to the ground at the feet of the great lord. Everyone assumed that he would now be impaled on a stake, or perhaps hanged like a dog from a well-pole. None was more certain of this than the poor Qangli himself, for his negligence had been a great negligence. When they pushed him to the ground he simply crumpled, as though the body beneath his cloak was entirely without bones.

'Take the iron off his leg!'

The Qangli did not understand—perhaps did not even really hear—and was only prompted to action by a few solid kicks from the leading Hun's boot. He unfastened the iron bar from Kung's leg.

'You're free!' said the Hun.

The envoy of the Son of Heaven suspected a ruse.

'Do not think, young warrior, that kindness will win for you what you could not obtain through force. There are many, of course, who withstood the red-hot irons of cruelty, only to succumb to the sweet rose of mercy. But know this: neither good nor ill treatment shall draw from me the secret I possess. I shall never betray what was entrusted to me.'

'You're free,' the Hun repeated.

'And you think that this will make me give up my secret? No! Neither the sweet honeycomb nor the torturer's bench! I shall never give up the Emperor's secret!'

The Hun leader shook his head contemptuously.

'Keep it. Who cares? It doesn't matter any more. A secret

from thirty years ago? What good is that to anyone? You're free. You can go where you please. Do you understand? You're free.'

Kung staggered, his eyes wild and baffled. He ran a trembling hand over his face and up across his bald pate, then looked around as though coming to with a start.

Beside him lay the long iron bar with its chain still attached. He lifted it, the rattling chain swinging back and forth, and leant his weight on it.

Then, without a word of thanks or goodbye, he set off. He walked between the gaping barbarians, speaking to nobody. Not to the Massagetean farmer, nor even to the Qangli guard. Not to anyone.

Not a word.

He headed east, towards his home, to where the first hint of dawn split earth and sky with a faint band of rosy pink. They watched him for a long time, a limping silhouette against the steppe horizon, the heavy iron bar held like a crutch in his crippled hand.

His ragged, weatherbeaten form faded by degrees into the dawn's gathering haze, until at last he was entirely lost to sight.

WOLVES

Winter. Snow fell heavily upon the hills and valleys of Transylvania and upon the high-domed, thatched cottages of the Vlach[8] peasants. It fell upon the rocky mountainsides, softening their jagged ridges, and strewed the deep forest interiors with numberless glistering diamonds. The normal confusion of earth, rocks and weeds lay hidden beneath the falling flakes, and the Maros valley was transformed into an unbroken expanse of purest white.

Only in the Hungarian-speaking villages by the banks of the Maros did the dark patches begin to appear: burned, blackened timbers, and the charred branches of poplars reaching skyward like upturned, sooty brooms. The few houses still standing had no roofs, and their walls were canted at strange angles.

And from the empty village streets to the castles and manor houses that dotted the surrounding countryside, all was shrouded in dead, utter silence.

Still the snow fell, blowing through broken windows and thatchless eaves, half filling the interiors, or, where brick arches still stood, sifting in diagonal ridges of ever-finer flakes. Here and there on house walls or tree trunks were strange, dark-crimson stains, frozen to icy pools. Snow covered everything except these dark pools; any white flakes which fell on them were soon blown away.

Amid the blackened pines of former gardens, and out in the nearby fields, a visitor would have seen long, narrow rectangles of raised snow which marked the fresh graves. Each had been sniffed at, dug up and quarrelled over by hungry dogs. Whenever a body was unearthed, a cloud of rooks, jackdaws and carrion crows would descend upon it in a bickering throng.

1785 was a winter of ghastly silence, quieter by far than any other winter, as though life itself had been reduced to a feeble flicker, and mankind was barely to be found.

1785 was a winter of ghastly silence, for it was the winter after Horea's Revolt.

And from remote mountain fastnesses came wolves, prowling round every hamlet and isolated farmstead. At first they came only in ones and twos, but as winter bit hard and the snow piled up they began to hunt in ever-larger packs.

They came at dusk or in the dead of night, padding noiselessly along the tree line in single file. In appearance they were not so very remarkable—a casual observer might have taken them, in repose, for a pack of unkempt sheepdogs —but no dogs possess their calm, watchful patience.

A dangerous patience. They would strike only when it was very dark, and even then there was no commotion. The farmer would simply discover at dawn that one of his ewes was gone. No trace ever remained, besides fresh blood on the snow. They always came at night, like careful thieves, and nothing seemed to stop them. In vain the shepherds shivered through the night in thick cloaks, or posted big, brave dogs to guard their flocks. One such dog was even torn to pieces in the night, without anybody hearing a thing.

The county sheriff offered a reward of two silver pieces for each wolf-head—a lot of money in those days—but though the news spread all through the mountains, few were ever caught. Besides, there was game in those forests worth far more than the elusive wolves. Horea and Cloșca, two leaders of the revolt, had already been brought to Gyulafehérvár in chains, with three hundred gold pieces paid for each. Now the mountains were being scoured for Horea's deputy, Gavril Lung, worth two hundred gold pieces dead or alive.

The wolves prowled in peace.

It was late afternoon, and a ragged, ash-grey band climbed the Szamos valley, from Toszerát towards the distant peak of the Humpleu. They walked silently, in single file, with old Maftei in the lead. Maftei, the owner of the Toszerát sawmill, was a short, dog-faced man of late middle-age. He was the guide.

Behind him walked Dumitru Niag, a *gornyik* or forest warden, with a musket slung over one shoulder. A peaked lambskin cap indicated his superior social rank, and the rags on his back were strung with blue braid. He was evidently the leader. Behind him came two men from the village of Gyurkuca: skinny Pantilimon and Simion son of Avram. Last of all came the younger Maftei, a shepherd boy from Mereggyó whom everyone called 'Cock Robin'.

All were burdened with provisions for the road, and wore old-fashioned cloaks of black haircloth over their ragged clothes. The four peasants wore identical dress and only the tall warden's clothes showed any ornamentation. Aside from the blue braid, he carried an elegant satchel in several colours, and a leather knapsack on his back. He was also the only man armed with a gun; the others all had long-handled axes.

They pushed on towards the Humpleu, kicking through drifts of virgin snow. Their rawhide moccasins were thick with snow, and their trousers white to the knee. Firmer sections would give a sighing creak before giving way beneath old Maftei's tread. Their footsteps left a long, low trench in the white snow, its sides steel-grey in the winter light.

Reaching the Poieni meadows, old Maftei the guide stopped and pointed his axe-handle towards the pine forest on the valley's far side. Seven wolves were moving along the tree line in single file, at about the same pace as the men.

They too were heading towards the Humpleu.

'Worth fourteen of his Majesty's[9] best,' he said with a grin.

'Don't count your chickens,' growled Dumitru Niag, the warden with the musket.

'Come on.'

They went on as wordlessly as before, ascending the lowermost slopes of the Humpleu and still shadowed a little way off by the wolves, until at last they left the meadows and entered the strange world of the great forests…

It was long after dark by the time they reached the summit, and by then three men had fallen behind. Maftei and Cock Robin were alone as they walked towards the cauldron-shaped hollow on the Humpleu's cratered peak. In the centre of this hollow—chosen because its rocky walls hid any light—a fire burned. Beside it, sitting in the entrance to an improvised shack, a young man gazed listlessly into the flames, a musket cradled in his lap.

Before he even reached the lip of the rocky concavity, old Maftei called out in a loud, clear voice.

'It's Maftei! I've brought the cheese!'

It was only with great difficulty that the old man, burdened as he was, managed to descend the snow-covered rocks; he was out of breath by the time he reached the bottom. Cock Robin followed slowly, planting his feet precisely in the footsteps of the man in front.

Reaching the fire, Maftei slumped down next to it with an old man's customary grunts and groans. He spoke no greeting, but simply unslung the black striped bag from his shoulder and flung it to the ground as though he bore it some particular grudge.

'There's the cheese, Gavril Lung.'

'Why did you bring the boy?' Gavril asked darkly, jutting his chin towards Cock Robin.

Maftei just grimaced and stretched out his tired legs, so Lung repeated the question.

'Wolves, lad, wolves,' Maftei said at last, then began to speak in a manner quite unlike his usual taciturn self. He gave a detailed, impassioned account of a wolf attack the night before, in which his finest cow had been torn to pieces right next to the barn. There had been no sound, and not even the dogs had barked. He heaped foul curses upon both the wolves and his dogs, calling on God to shrivel their useless, silent throats. Wolves. Too many wolves, and they had left no more of his precious cow than would fit in the palm of one hand. They had come just before dawn, when he was still in bed, but he had heard their howls. So engrossed was he in the tale that he gave three long cries in imitation. Or was it a signal? Because whether by accident or design, his three companions appeared at that moment at the lip of the hollow. There was Dumitru Niag, the *gornyik*, and the two men from Gyurkuca, Pantilimon and Simion.

Gavril went to lift his musket, but Cock Robin, perhaps accidentally, had sat down on it.

'Who are they? Maftei! Who are those men?'

'Hunters. Wolf hunters. They came up with me,' Maftei answered calmly. He spat into the fire and it sputtered.

The newcomers, descending very slowly and deliberately by the same route, approached the fire and greeted Gavril with formal courtesy:

'God grant you good evening.'

Then they sat down around the fire with as many grunts and groans as old Maftei. Next to Gavril was Dumitru with his musket, while on the far side sat Cock Robin, then the two Gyurkuca men and Maftei.

Gavril and Dumitru, the *gornyik*, were both from the same village, up near the source of the Aranyos.

'Is that you, Mitru?' asked Gavril. 'What are you doing here?'

'Better off up here than in the lowlands. Can't move for soldiers down there.'

Conversation began slowly, punctuated with long, pensive silences. Now and then someone would rake the fire with a stick, sending a galaxy of sparks spiralling upwards through the smoke. It was late, but Gavril still seemed wary. He spoke only occasionally, and his right hand remained tucked inside his jacket where the chased silver butts of two elegant French pistols were just visible. Not that there was anything particularly suspicious in the behaviour of these men; they took supplies out of their haversacks, then unwound their sopping footwraps and held them towards the fire to dry. A pipe was passed round, and though they spoke only in the gruff monotone of the mountains, their conversation grew gradually more cheerful. Soldiers, they said, were in Topánfalva, with many more in Albák and some even as far off as Felsőaranyos. Shaking his head, Maftei told how each family was expected to provision them with two pats of butter.

'It's a hard station for the likes of us,' he said.

Time passed, and as they spoke they passed round a little flask of strong drink. Only the *gornyik* Dumitru never spoke, but merely grunted or shook his head occasionally. His eyes strayed frequently to the hand Gavril kept in the breast of his jacket, and the two protruding pistol butts.

Maftei lifted a log from the woodpile and set it on the fire, but this upset the delicate structure and it collapsed in a shower of sparks. A burning log rolled down near Gavril's feet, filling the air around him with smoke. He bent down to toss it back.

That was his mistake, leaning over and taking his eyes off the men next to him. Cock Robin and Dumitru were on him in a flash, with the two Gyurkuca men, Pantilimon and Simion, joining them a few seconds later. Only Maftei remained where he stood, peering through the smoke at the scrum on the far side of the fire, but moving no closer.

When they had Gavril pinned down they took his pistols from him and kicked his musket a few feet away. Then Dumitru Niag went over to his haversack and pulled out a set of iron chains wrapped in cloth, which he fixed on Gavril's wrists and one ankle. He worked with calm, professional efficiency, and when he was finished they all sat down around the fire again, panting. Neither they nor their captive spoke; Gavril simply stared at them with blazing eyes and breathed heavily, like a wounded boar at bay.

Silence fell once more around the fire, as though nothing at all had happened; the chains and the trampled snow behind Gavril were the only signs that an altercation had taken place. The pipe was relit, and snow-chilled, calloused hands were held palm-out towards the fire. Conversation began again, and they spoke gruffly about taxes, and wolves, and the hard winter, spitting intermittently into the fire as before.

A little later Gavril cleared his throat.

'I'm cold. Bring me closer to the fire.'

They pulled him closer. Now Dumitru turned to Gavril, as though to cheer him up, and said that Horea and Cloşca had been caught by six of his *gornyik* colleagues in just the same way. Sitting next to them by the fire, they had waited for their moment to pounce. It was exactly the same.

This seemed to interest Gavril, and perhaps even to calm him a little: the news that his superiors had fallen into the same trap was some consolation.

'And Urs Uibar? And Crişan? What happened to them? Have they been caught?'

His captors spoke in turn, telling him what they knew about his former companions. They were polite and deferential, implicitly recognising him as a man of consequence, and as time went by they seemed to forget that they had ever leapt upon him, clapping him in irons to deliver him to the hangman the next day. Even Gavril seemed to relax a little, and smiled ruefully at their coarse peasant jokes. Once or twice he even laughed.

With time they grew gradually quieter; one or two men dozed off, and the others gazed out blankly into the blue-black depths of the forest. Only the fire still crackled with ceaseless vigour. Then over its low snapping there came another sound. From somewhere far off came a long, drawn-out howl. It was an eerie, hair-raising sound, seeming to reach them not through the air but through the ground at their feet. It came again, then a third time.

Wolves.

Cock Robin was the first to hear it, and leapt to his feet. Pantilimon and Simion also rose. Nobody moved, and they all listened in silence until at last old Maftei spoke.

'Not far off. And coming closer.'

Dumitru nodded.

'It would be an easy thing to make a few silver crowns if I had the eyes of a younger man,' said Maftei. 'And a gun.' He stared straight ahead as though speaking to the fire, but his words were plainly directed at Dumitru.

'Can anyone call?' asked Dumitru.

Wolf hunting takes at least two, one to shoot and one to call, but almost all the mountain men could imitate a wolf call in those days. Tall Pantilimon cupped his hands over his mouth and let out a long, low wail, the veins on his thin neck standing out like cables.

Satisfied with this performance, Dumitru nodded. At Maftei's encouragement the others joined them, and Dumitru, Pantilimon, Simion and Cock Robin prepared to set off into the forest.

'I'm too old for that sort of thing,' said Maftei with a sigh. 'And someone has to make sure Gavril here makes no trouble.'

His voice was tired and a little sad as though dispirited by this reminder of his advancing years. The others set off.

Along the ridge connecting the Humpleu and the Muncel Mare, seven wolves trotted in single file. The lead wolf, a big reddish-brown animal, loped through the snow at a steady pace, nose close to the ground and tail down. When he stopped the others stopped, looking around with their ears pricked before setting off again.

Then they heard the wolf-call, from the direction of the Humpleu's summit. The wolves stopped, but for a long time there was only silence. Then at last it came again. They set off towards it, the big red wolf in the lead, but even more cautiously than before. Again they heard it, closer now, and straight up the hillside. The lead wolf slowed a little, licking his lips in perplexity. What was it about that call that sounded just a little peculiar? Had it really been a wolf?

They came to a clearing, and the lead wolf stopped at the tree line. From behind a low pine branch he gazed apprehensively at the space beyond. It was so bright out there! So exposed. The virgin snow beyond shone pale in the pre-dawn light. Nothing had crossed it all night. After hesitating for a long time he stepped forward into the open.

A musket banged.

Who can calculate the infinitesimal span of a single moment? Yet how much can occur within one! The instant before the shot rang out he saw the hunters. Though unable to dodge the shot entirely, he had twisted aside, and the bullet did not quite hit square on. The other wolves fled.

He spun, snarling, to where his thigh had exploded in pain, then ran after his companions. Together, all seven fled back through the forest the way they had come. They still moved in single file, following their old course and leaving hardly any new tracks. Only here and there did a crimson drop from the flank of the big male fall to leave a tiny stain upon the colourless snow. They vanished into the darkness.

Maftei was silent. His feet rested against a rotten log, and his bloodshot, heavy-lidded eyes stared into the flickering depths of the fire. He watched as the golden-bodied flames leapt and danced, their tips green and blue against the silhouetted pines. He placed another branch on the fire and watched as the flames crept along the lichen-covered bark, as though the wood itself were fulfilling some innate, cathartic urge towards self-immolating apotheosis. Here and there, like the vents of a great forge, deeper fissures would send forth flickering flames of purest cobalt. At last the great branch would sputter and fume, then slowly split asunder like a pair of fiery red lips. Like a smile from the chasms of hell. Later the fire would catch some dry twig, bituminous with sap, which would flare up in a great, brief blaze entirely disproportionate to its size, illuminating with fresh clarity the features of Maftei's fireside companion.

Gavril too was silent. Ever since the others had gone, leaving him alone with this dog-faced old man, the reality of his captivity had begun to weigh upon him, as did the chains on his wrists. A vague childhood memory arose in his mind of the time he had seen a man dragged to the gallows in Gyulafehérvár; it seemed impossible that he should ever be that same man. Gavril did not speak, but tears clouded his vision and a low moan escaped his lips.

After a long pause, Maftei spoke.

'So you were in charge at Topánfalva?'

He said no more but Gavril understood that he was talking about the raid on the money-lender's house, where a large store of gold had been taken.

'Why?'

'Just asking.'

'Well, I was. Why?'

'Just asking,' Maftei repeated nonchalantly, then spat into the fire.

They were silent again, and neither moved. Gavril sensed that Maftei had some question in mind which he was reluctant to ask. Maftei did indeed speak again, but without taking his eyes off the fire.

'Fine day's work, that…'

'It was.'

Maftei muttered something inaudible and stirred the fire with a stick. He frowned, evidently turning over some thought. At last he looked up, but not before spitting into the fire again as though to reassure himself.

'What would you give me if I set you free?'

Hope suddenly blazed afresh in Gavril's breast. It was the hope of freedom, though he took care not to show it. In fact, though decades younger than Maftei, his expression was as inscrutable as the older man's. He grunted.

'Five gold pieces,' he said, then decided to add an extra proof of his generosity. 'And a piglet at Easter.'

The old man did not answer. Picking up another branch, he placed it on the fire and spent a long time making sure that it caught properly. He put his hand in among the flames to adjust its position, and anyone would have thought he would be badly burned, but he moved quickly, and his calloused old palms could stand the heat.

'I'd give you more!'

Motionless, the old man just stared into the blazing fire, chin jutting forward and his teeth clenched. There was something utterly merciless in that grizzled, dog-like face, and in that long mouth with its thin, colourless lips. His small, dark, deep-set eyes were unreadable.

'A lot more! Say twice that! Ten pieces of gold!' There was no more talk of the piglet.

Maftei did not reply.

Hope swelled within Gavril, ever more unbearably, like a stone in his throat. He knew that time was passing, and that sooner or later the others would be back. This was his last chance.

'Come on Maftei, tell me! How much do you want?'

Far off they heard the crack of a gunshot. Gavril knew now that the others would be back before long.

'Maftei, listen Maftei, I'll give a lot more, all right? Come on, tell me Maftei, how much do you want? Half? You want half? You can have it! Tell me, is that enough? Half?'

He stared anxiously into the sawmill owner's face, which

glowed red in the firelight. At last the old man answered.

'How do I even know how much half is?'

'You don't, and neither do I, but it's a lot! A fortune! Look, we'll split it together, in person, but first just let me out of these chains! We'll split it in person!'

'Hm. Good.'

'Good! But unchain me quickly! We've already heard a shot, so it won't be long until they're back!'

Maftei, however, would not be rushed.

'First tell me where it is.'

'Unchain me and I'll show you.'

Maftei shook his head.

'No. Tell me first. I'm an old man and you're a young lad. I can't catch you if you run.'

Gavril hesitated, but his native caution was still too strong.

'No. I can't tell you first.'

'Suit yourself,' said the dog-faced old man, spitting into the fire as a sign that it was all the same to him.

They were silent again. Every nerve, every pore of Gavril's skin quivered in anxious expectation of footsteps in the distance. Were they coming? Fear coursed through him, and a savage yearning to be free. Again he saw in his mind that big gallows in the market square of Gyulafehérvár. The memory was not vague at all now, but as clear as if he were standing right before it. He saw the withered, formless things hanging on ropes below the crossbeam, and the boys throwing stones at them. Each impact made a dull, hollow thunk, as though the dangling corpses had been carved from wood. It was that, the peculiar thunk, that somehow appalled him most of all.

He sat in silence, trying to hear over the roaring pulse in his ears whether the others were coming. Every time the dawn breeze rustled in the trees, every time a branch cracked in the fire, a wave of cold dread washed over him. Still he listened, knowing how precious each second was.

At last he could take no more, and cleared his throat.

'The spring by the Gruiu Ursului. By the big, white pine, facing towards the beech tree. I etched a cross on one of the roots; it's under there.' He spoke quickly and precisely, his voice so low it was almost a whisper. 'Now unchain me, quickly!'

The old man got lugubriously to his feet, but did not approach Gavril. Instead he hefted his axe and walked over to a fallen tree twenty paces or so away, where he cut off two or three branches. Then, with perhaps exaggerated signs of age and fatigue, he dragged one back towards the fire, the branches cutting long furrows in the snow. Sitting by the fire once more, he began chopping it into smaller pieces.

Gavril, beside himself, called out again and again, panic edging his voice.

'Maftei! Maftei! Unchain me! Maftei!'

The old man paid no heed. Supplication and entreaty mixed with furious curses, but Maftei seemed as little to notice as if he had that instant been struck deaf. With calm, complacent ease he cut the long branch into pieces. Then, after driving the axe head into a nearby stump, he began carefully placing cut logs onto the fire, arranging them with those grizzled hands. He never so much as glanced towards Gavril, who flailed in his chains and howled the most incoherent curses.

'Bastard! You bastard!'

Old Maftei's features could have been carved from stone. Neither sorrow nor satisfied revenge nor wicked glee shone there, just the same blank, unreadable expression as ever.

At length the trees rustled, the snow crunched, and voices sounded from beyond the camp-fire. The others were returning, and though Gavril's heart still pounded violently in his chest, he fell silent.

They descended by the same route they had come, following their own tracks. The only difference was that now they were six instead of five: the shackled Gavril followed at the rear. They walked in single file, as wordlessly as on the ascent. All were entirely alike in their silence, their clothes, their long strides and even their blank, unreadable expressions. Without the chains on Gavril's wrists, it would have been impossible to tell the prisoner from the guards.

Reaching the banks of the Szamos, they paused to rest. That was where Maftei unexpectedly announced that he would not accompany them on to Topánfalva. It was bad, he said, to leave the sawmill unattended for so long.

Before parting, and with Gavril still standing next to them, they bargained for who should get what from the reward. It was agreed that everyone should get fifteen pieces of gold, with another fifteen for Dumitru, the leader, and another ten for Maftei, who had guided them to their quarry. This took some time, since Maftei tried to bargain for more, though the amounts had been agreed in advance. Gavril listened to all this without apparent interest, as though it were not his own life they were bargaining over.

The business at last settled, Dumitru, Pantilimon, Simion, Cock Robin and Gavril set off, heading across the Gialu Boului towards Albák and Topánfalva, where they would hand over their captive and collect their reward.

Old Maftei still sat by the banks of the Szamos, waiting until the others had disappeared into the forest on the river's far bank. He waited patiently, his chin raised as though sniffing the air. Gavril looked back twice, but both times he saw the old man still sitting motionless on the stone, legs spread in front of him. Only when the others had vanished from view did he at last set off, and not towards the sawmill; instead he went back up the hillside, cutting diagonally across in the direction of the Gruiu Ursului. He was heading for the white pine near the spring. Moving at a steady, stubborn, unhurried pace, he made his way up the bare hillside, until he too disappeared amid the pines.

Towards evening, seven wolves came down from the Humpleu about a mile and a half away. Six moved in single file, going at a steady, loping pace, while the seventh lagged some way behind. A drop of blood occasionally fell on the snow where the seventh walked, but only a single drop. They reached the edge of the woods and saw a flock of sheep grazing on the pastures below. It was still too light to risk an attack, so they sat down in a ragged line to wait. Their twitching nostrils sniffed the chill evening air, and occasionally they scratched at fleas. Decorum was, as ever among wolves, at a minimum.

The big male sat down a little way off from the others. His tongue lolled and he was panting for breath; the climb had tired him, but the others showed no sign of noticing. He often turned to lick at his wounded hindquarters.

Then one of the other wolves rose and came towards him. He sniffed, and though the bigger wolf growled he did not move away. Instead he came closer, carefully scrutinising the patch of dry blood on his back leg. Now two more padded silently over, so that three pairs of hard, green eyes were fixed upon him in cold, measured contemplation.

Night fell, and as the sky turned a deeper shade of grey, the pale wolf eyes took on a steelier resolve. Four, five, six pairs of eyes. The big wolf growled quietly, putting his head down between his front paws then suddenly turning on them with a vicious snarl, teeth glinting in the darkness. The others did not move, just watched with cold, green, hungry eyes…

It was pitch dark now, and six wolves crossed the tree line onto the open pastures. They moved in single file, leaving only one set of tracks in the snow. Crossing that white expanse, they were like the shadows of *komondor*[10] sheepdogs. Now and then they stopped, ears twitching, then padded on…

Back at the tree line where they had waited all evening, a large pool of blood stained the compressed snow. Further off lay scattered clumps of fur—wolf fur—and beyond that the head of the big male. The lower jaw was half buried in the snow, mouth wide and teeth still bared in a snarl, glassy eyes staring with cold fury at the moonlit night…

THE INFECTED PLANET

I once took a trip to Scotland, at the invitation of a certain John Paton. He was a great lover of all things Hungarian, having spent most of the Great War as a prisoner in Transylvania, where he was treated, by all accounts, more like the village guest of honour than a prisoner, and the experience proved so agreeable that he returned many times in later years. It was during one of these visits that he invited me to Scotland on a shooting trip, where our quarry was to be that quintessential Scottish game bird, the grouse.

The red grouse, a type of ptarmigan, is a close relative of the willow grouse but can be differentiated by its lack of winter plumage. The species is unique to the British Isles. I have certainly never encountered it anywhere else. It is also an excellent game bird, flying in such unpredictable zig-zags, and at speeds rivalling the snipe, that it takes all a sportsman's skill and concentration to bring one down. These birds feed almost exclusively on heather, and so are found in the wildest, most barren parts of the Scottish Highlands. There, however, they are abundant, and a group of guns might bag as many as forty or fifty in a single drive.

Scotland will always remain for me a most happy memory. Crossing the border, I sensed at once that we were entering another country. All the way from London to Northumberland the houses are built almost exclusively of red brick, with matching red roof tiles. It was these, set against the marvellous oak trees, fields and hedgerows of rural England, which led one French writer to remark that the English countryside resembles nothing so much as a 'plate of gammon and spinach, all bright reds and greens.' Crossing the border, however, we entered another world entirely. Here the houses are built of pale granite and roofed in dark-grey slate. Scotland is also much more sparsely inhabited than England, and we crossed many desolate moors without seeing so much as a single farm.

It teems, however, with historical lore, and my host's stories about this or that landmark made a deep impression on me as we drove north.

'This is the town Banquo came from, and see those ruined ramparts? That's Dunsinane, the castle of Macbeth.'

'And Birnam Wood?'

'That was further on, round the bend of this valley. She'll come no more to high Dunsinane, though; those woods were cut down centuries ago. It's all pastureland now.'

He said all this with the nonchalant matter-of-factness we might use to describe the cattle fair at Mócs, or a tavern in Mezőbánd[11]. How peculiar, I thought, that what for more distant readers of Shakespeare seems a world almost of fairy tale and make-believe is here a tangible reality, graspable by simply looking out of the window. All the scene lacked were three witches round a bubbling cauldron, though perhaps they too remain, transmogrified by time into dinner party hostesses and the wives of steel barons or ironmasters, their hair glistening with bright diamonds instead of snakes.

We drove north from Perth into the true highlands, and I can hardly describe the gladdening effect this landscape had on my Transylvanian heart. To the last detail it seemed a facsimile of the Mezőség, that broad expanse of bare, upland pasture east of Kolozsvár. Here too, treeless hills stretch towards the horizon, broken by rock-sided valleys. Occasionally I saw grouse-shooting butts: low, semi-circular shelters built without mortar from the blocks of granite which lie scattered in every direction. The underlying geology is almost the only real difference between the Scottish Highlands and the Mezőség: these hills are all granite, while ours are clay. Still, the rock was only visible on the most precipitous cliffs; grass and heather cloaked every other surface. It was early autumn, and the blooming heather lent every hillside a glorious, shimmering iridescence which varied from deep purple to flame-red depending on the light, and stretched from the highest peak to the boggy brooks or 'burns' which gurgled along the valley floors.

On each succeeding morning, as I stood alone in my butt, it was all too easy to imagine myself back on the high Rücsi, or in those hay meadows facing the Nagycég on the lower slopes of the Fundáta, when the wildflowers are at their freshest and loveliest.

Pleasant daydreams.

During the shoot I made the acquaintance of a very likeable gentleman whose name, if I remember correctly, was McPherson. Sir Something-or-other McPherson, to be precise, where the 'Something-or-other' stands in for a long-forgotten first name and the 'Sir' indicates that he was a knight.

This McPherson was a big, heavy-set man, and no longer young; he must have been in his fifties at least. He was, however, a remarkable shot, and I rarely saw him miss. By the standards of the British gentry he would not have been considered wealthy, living as he did in a modest but very pretty little house not far from Aberdeen. It was surrounded by a charming flower garden, and commanded views of the rolling Eastern Highlands.

He was excellent company, with the sort of loud, jovial good humour I so often encountered in Scotland. Nothing pleased him more than a funny story, and his own were accompanied by grand, sweeping gestures and hearty laughter. He had spent most of his career as an official in East Africa. In what capacity? Well, it was almost too strange to believe: he had been chief warden for some vast swathe of the Kenyan Serengeti, responsible not for the local inhabitants but for the wild animals. His task had been to keep an eye on the zebra, gazelle, lions and so on, protecting the ones which seemed in difficulty and putting down any that caused mischief. He ultimately became both a caretaker and a sort of policemen among the animals of the African bush. If, for instance, his subordinates told him of a lion which, growing old and slow, was no longer able to catch prey—not even an unarmed man, which is the easiest prey of all—and so was pitifully wasting away, he would go out with his rifle and shoot it. His authority extended over all animals, and he made sure they were protected from pests and poachers, while also managing population numbers. He showed me a photograph of a particular bull elephant with only one tusk. Such elephants, he told me, are extremely dangerous to the rest of the herd, not only because they are perpetually bad-tempered and worry the calves and females, but because of what happens in a duel between two bulls. Ordinarily, the tusks serve both an offensive and a defensive purpose but a one-tusked elephant often fatally wounds a rival, since instead of locking horns with his opponent, his single tusk slides between the other elephant's two and buries itself in the soft flesh of the trunk. The elephant in the photograph was one such case: the loss of his tusk meant that he had to be destroyed.

The photograph was extremely interesting. It showed the beast just as he was turning to charge, huge ears splayed and dust rising from where he had stamped the dry earth. McPherson could only have been thirty paces away when he snapped the picture, before hefting his hunting rifle and shooting that enormous quarry between the eyes.

He certainly had the most extraordinary sang-froid.

The skull of this particular elephant, with one tusk and a small hole in the middle of the forehead, was mounted in McPherson's living room. I went over to take a closer look, and found that great ivory blade as sharp as the antlers on a Transylvanian red deer.

All this was both fascinating and unfamiliar. The idea that the British passion for order should extend not only to the multifarious human inhabitants of their vast empire, but even to the wild animals which chanced to live there, was so bizarre that I hardly knew what to say. Still, if they really considered it their responsibility to ensure the welfare of all creatures under their dominion then I supposed that was splendid.

Perhaps my long pondering of this question explains the dream I had that night. In fact, the truth is that I cannot now be sure whether it was really a dream or a sort of vision. Or perhaps I just imagined the whole thing. I really do not know.

It was pitch dark, without the merest scintilla of light. I had the impression that there was no solid surface anywhere; I seemed to be floating in a featureless void, like Adam before the Creation in Madách's *The Tragedy of Man*[12]. I, however, was utterly alone, without even Lucifer for company. So appalling was the thought of my absolute solitude that I confess even the devil would have been a comfort. But no, nothing.

Nothing.

This continued for what seemed an eternity, until at long, long last there came a sound. From somewhere far off I heard the murmur of voices. How? Where? I have no idea, but there it was, coming from a long way off.

At first it was barely audible, like a soft and very distant whisper, and completely incomprehensible. Then it slowly began to grow louder, or perhaps my ears simply grew more accustomed to the faint sound. I strained to hear what was being said, and words gradually began to emerge from the indistinct mumble, until by degrees I found myself catching the drift of whole sentences

'I performed a full orbit, just as instructed,' a voice was saying. 'An orbital inspection. That's why I have summoned the council. The results are extremely disturbing and there is no question that something must be done. One of the planets is very unwell indeed.'

'Which one?' asked a grave, officious voice, perhaps the chair.

'Third from the sun, the pretty little blue one with the single moon. I can't think of any planet so lush and verdant for light-years around, and in this particular quadrant it's my definite favourite. Its oceans teem with life, while forests cover much of the dry land. Now, though, it seems the greater portion will likely turn to barren desert.'

'Are you quite certain of that?' asked a new voice.

'I'm afraid so. Not trusting my own judgement in this matter, I asked the quadrant's chief medical officer for his opinion. He conducted a thorough investigation and the results…well, perhaps I should let him tell you himself, since it's his professional domain.'

'Thank you, yes, quite so,' said another new voice, presumably the medical officer. 'It's a sad but indubitable fact, gentlemen, that the planet has been infected by a parasitic micro-organism. If one observes the land through a magnifying lens it becomes clear that the greater part of the forest cover has already been lost. Only around the equator and in the sub-polar regions do the forests remain more or less intact. In temperate regions they have practically disappeared, while calciferous, rocky cankers have sprung up everywhere, particularly in coastal regions and along the banks of larger rivers. Now, observe these rocky outgrowths more carefully and you will see that they are positively crawling with the little beasts that made them. What is more, they seem to be multiplying at a terrific rate, and linking their colonies together with a network of trails, so that new sites of infection are springing up all the time. My diagnosis, I'm afraid, is that this planet has been infected by anthropoides, causing that rare but extremely dangerous condition known as anthropocitis.'

'No! How appalling!' Several voices called out at once.

'I agree entirely. Appalling. The cause, specifically, appears to be a small bipedal organism which the untrained observer might easily mistake for one of the planet's forest-dwelling apes. Apes and their smaller cousins, monkeys, are, however, entirely benign, while their near relative the human, agglomerating in permanent colonies sometimes several million strong, is perhaps the most grievous infestation known to science. There is, at present, no known cure.'

'But I mean, surely we have to do something? Does the chief superintendent have any advice? I remember a few eons ago we went to considerable pains to make sure this little planet was in good health.'

Now the first voice spoke again.

'Quite true. Back then I also took the liberty of summoning the council, when the signs of infection were still incipient. The council, you may recall, decided upon a great flood, so I melted the poles and washed the land with a great deluge. At first we were confident that—though at great collateral cost—we had at least succeeded in curing the anthropocitis. With time, lush rainforests sprang up again, and I was ready to give the place a clean bill of health. You can imagine my consternation when it became clear that this appalling infection had in fact persisted.'

'I see. Well, perhaps if we tried again…'

'No, that won't work now. At that time they had one big sea-going vessel of which, alas, I was unaware. Now they have thousands of the things, and even if hurricanes and whirlpools sunk the greater part, some would undoubtedly survive. After a few millennia we would be back to square one.

'I see. And an ice age?'

Now the medical officer spoke.

'The polar climate doesn't seem to cause it any great harm. Anthropoides is, if you like, clever enough to adapt, and makes shelters against the cold. We can be sure of this, since though we were unaware of its existence then, the infection must already have been present during the last ice age, and survived without great difficulty.'

'Nothing! Nothing can stop this appalling rot! My poor heart will break, watching this little jewel of a planet slowly wither. Absolutely atrocious!'

The chief superintendent's voice caught, as though choking back a sob.

Now some previously silent member of the council spoke, his voice hard and grim.

'Look here, superintendent, if this slow decay will cause you such grief, surely better to exterminate the infected planet now! Bang! A puff of smoke, and you can put the sorry case from your mind. We have meteors for that sort of thing, after all, and I seem to recall we did the same thing to this planet's neighbour when it came down with a case of anthropocitis. Most of you are relatively new here in the Inner Milky Way, but I remember the whole affair. The debris still follows the old planet's orbit, circling the solar system between Mars and Jupiter and doing nobody any harm.'

The medical officer spoke.

'I'm afraid I cannot endorse this course of action, and indeed as a physician I must strongly caution against it. My predecessor, I know, allowed the last obliteration, but that may have been precisely how the germs spread as far as the Andromeda Nebula. The bacillus itself is easily killed, of course, but the spores are extraordinarily resistant to cold. Even absolute zero won't reliably denature them. I have, I fear, all-too-real grounds for suspecting that the destruction of this planet would only spread the disease to other planets, starting of course with the nearest ones, and the resultant cosmic dust could carry the seeds of life almost infinite distances through outer space. Nor can I agree that the Asteroid Belt does no harm; I for one find it a considerable hazard and nuisance when navigating this solar system. If we destroy this planet then we can look forward not only to a good deal more clutter and debris, but to the infection of those planets closest at hand, and perhaps even those in the Sirius or Orion systems as well. I ask that this warning be recorded in the minutes of this council meeting as my formal medical opinion, along with a note stating that I opposed planetary obliteration in the strongest possible terms.'

Anger rose in the medical officer's voice as he spoke, and by the end he sounded positively furious. Now, however, the chairman spoke, his voice full of calm wisdom.

'Never fear, professor; no need for that. We all defer to your expertise in such matters. It seems to me that the most prudent course of action is to refrain from any violent intervention for now, and to let events take their course. I'm no expert, of course, but I've heard it said that these anthropoides generally begin to destroy themselves when they multiply beyond a certain threshold. Dividing into mutually hostile populations, they kill one another in the most bewildering variety of ways, even producing poison gas to destroy their own kind in greater numbers. Isn't that correct, professor?'

The medical officer concurring, the chairman went on.

'Our most recent, detailed observations seem to show considerable destruction to certain of their settlements. In the absence of large-scale volcanic eruptions or other natural events, the most likely explanation must be that these creatures did it to themselves. Things seem to have calmed recently, but perhaps there might be some way of rekindling their conflict? Does the professor perhaps know of some means to make their internecine squabbles more violent and deadly than ever?'

'Experiments seem to indicate that increasing the number and intensity of sunspots has some effect. It makes them more quarrelsome and excitable. We have only been able to test this in the lab, of course, but results so far seem consistent and replicable.'

'Really? Well, that would be something!'

'Yes. If we were able to replicate it on a planetary scale it would be splendid. Under the influence of these sunspots they gather in mutually hostile agglomerations tens of millions strong, then fire little lumps of iron at one another through tubes. It's a fascinating spectacle and causes quite a racket. We haven't determined yet how it's done, but one theory is that they eat the iron and then some explosive chemical reaction accompanies the excretion of their faeces. The improbably high readings of ferrous material in the cankerous colonies they live in seem to me to support this hypothesis. For this reason, our experiments always proved most effective when conducted on iron-rich ground. Then they usually end up attacking one another with such ferocity that before long hardly any are left alive.'

'Why, this is wonderful news! It sounds like just the thing! I shall take care of the sunspots, which should set them to killing one another again. Even if they don't wipe themselves out to the very last individual, their greatly reduced numbers will let primeval forest again blanket the land, with those rocky settlements swallowed once more beneath a canopy of fresh green leaves. Those blameless creatures which share the planet will once again have a rich habitat, and we may even hope that anthropoides itself will sink back into that simple, primate existence from which it so balefully emerged. Then at last there will be order, health, peace and quiet on that little planet.'

'Yes!'

'Wonderful!'

'I concur!'

There were shouts of acclamation from the assembled council members, and these hopeful voices, so full of benevolent confidence, were the last things I remember hearing. Did they fall silent, or did I fall asleep? Perhaps I woke up. I simply cannot say. One thing I am sure of: the next thing I knew I was lying in bed. It was a moment or two before I convinced myself that I was not in outer space, but in a charming little guest bedroom in Scotland. The smiling maid came in and pulled back the curtains.

I dressed quickly and went down to breakfast, which was as prodigious as any British breakfast ought to be. (Lunch, by contrast, is often a rather paltry affair of thin soup and cold sandwiches.) On the table were two varieties of local fish. One was that excellent white fish known in Hungary as 'spotted cod' but here as 'haddock', while the other was warm, fresh salmon from the local river. Besides this there were soft-boiled eggs in delightful little cups, and thinly sliced ham. The basis of any Scottish breakfast seems, however, to be a sort of hot, starchy oatmeal paste known as 'porridge'. It would be unfair to call it bad, exactly; the truth is it hardly tastes of anything at all, but I am sure it is terribly nutritious. The locals, at any rate, are very proud of it. I drank milky tea, ate my eggs and toast and spooned oat paste round my bowl, but was unable to join in my companions' jokes and rumbustious good-humour. My thoughts were preoccupied by the strange visions of the night before, and I could not free myself from them.

'Lord!' I thought. 'What mad rubbish a person dreams at night!'

SOMEWHERE

Who can say where this story takes place? It used to be that a person only had to mention the name of a country or city and anyone who had heard of it would know exactly where it was, as well as something about the general character of the place, and—in outline at least—what manner of people and society could be found there. Many, even if they had never been to such-and-such a place, knew much about it that was true, either by repute, through historical study or by familiarity with the characteristics of a certain nationality. Others had actually visited the place, though perhaps only briefly, and could at least call to mind some clear mental image. Still others had a great many memories to draw upon, perhaps the memories of long, heady, youthful journeys in which every recollection remained vivid and beautiful. For yet others, mention of a distant land might conjure up family, or a merry childhood spent in shaded gardens, among smiling, long-vanished faces. It meant 'home', with all the subtle magic that term implies.

Now everything has changed, and place names have lost their nimbus of associations. Now almost every name requires explanation, clarification, adjectives—which in any case scarcely help, since there is no inherent meaning to describe. Even geographical terms now define nothing in and of themselves and it is necessary to append some further remark, explaining whether such and such a place is new or old, or whether some familiar name encompasses an area broader or narrower than it once did. Expanded or contracted. And even if we succeed in summoning an image to go with a particular place, there is no guarantee that this will accord with the circumstances currently pertaining there. Mountain ranges still stand, impassive as ever, and rivers still flow in their prescribed channels, but the life of man is utterly, utterly changed.

For that reason we will delay no further in trying to define the country and city in which we presently find ourselves; it barely matters. The little story which follows might just as well be set anywhere in the world [13].

The tale concerns two English gentlemen, and begins with a large number of people gathered for luncheon. The host and hostess sit at opposite ends of the table, with the two English gentlemen placed next to the hostess.

One of these men, Mr Miller, was the British consul, and the city in which our story takes place had been his posting for two years. He was the son of the owner of 'Miller's Pills', that renowned manufacturer of indigestion tablets, and was extraordinarily wealthy. He viewed the diplomatic service chiefly as an interesting diversion, though he was not without idealism, and the notion of doing something for humanity's most miserable and impoverished souls appealed to him. Not that he dreamed of any great act of heroism, of course, but he did want to do *something*. He held it as a sacred duty incumbent upon everyone, and particularly upon an Englishman, to 'do one's bit'. Everyone doing one's bit was, he believed, the reason the Pound Sterling dominated the world's financial markets, and was the principle embodied in that bright little pennant, the Union Jack, which fluttered on the bonnet of his motorcar. He had a wrestler's physique, with enormous hands and a face like a block of granite, from which two watery blue eyes gazed upon the world with deliberate inscrutability. He sat on the hostess's right.

The second man was Major Bleuchamps, the local representative of the Anglo-Persian Oil Company. He sat on the hostess's left. Though the name might strike us as French, it was regarded in his homeland as thoroughly English, and had been pronounced 'Blutchem' for centuries. His family coat of arms—a blue shield with a tiny silver cross in the upper corner—could be found on one of the Crusader tombs in the Temple Church in London, while his uncle, His Grace the 7th Duke of Bleuchamps, had the ancient ancestral right to bear the monarch's glove at royal coronations.

He was a young man, considerably under thirty, and with his rosy cheeks and unlined forehead, few would even have guessed him to be more than twenty. He had been an officer in the Flying Corps during the war and, being entirely without a private fortune, had been forced to seek gainful employment after the armistice. The directors of the Anglo-Persian Oil Company had sent him here, to this remote backwater of Europe, to inspect a few sites suspected of containing significant deposits of oil. His job was to conduct a 'preliminary inspection', a difficult—perhaps impossible—task, for he knew of no means by which to peer unaided into the bowels of the earth. Still, the company expected him to give a full report on whether it was worthwhile sending an expensive expert to carry out further tests. That had been his job ever since the war, travelling to the most varied corners of the world and sending back his preliminary reports.

He had just spent three days walking through muddy, featureless fields, where now and again he had observed bubbles rising to the surface of opaque puddles before rupturing with a noxious burp. Occasionally he saw what looked like the remains of old boreholes in the clay. It was tiring, dirty work.

He was led to the place by the municipal commissioner for fiscal affairs and the district procurator, who shadowed his every step like prison guards. Neither had been able to tell him anything about the old drilling holes, or whether they had been dug by the state or by a private enterprise. That state would not have been the present state, after all, but the other one. The former one. Neither man seemed to consider it any business of his; when Bleuchamps asked them something about the activities of the former state they just shrugged. That was no surprise, and he knew that there was no point becoming frustrated with these people. Just a few years ago, after all, the municipal commissioner for fiscal affairs had been the school teacher in a remote mountain village which happened to have a salt mine—hence his secondment to the geology department—while the district procurator had been a barber in some German-speaking market town.

You could hardly expect much of such people.

Communication was also difficult, for though Bleuchamps had a smattering of German, the two men shadowing him barely seemed able to say a thing. It was a soul-destroying experience. He tried asking the local peasants, and though he eventually managed—at least to a degree—to overcome the language barrier, his inquiries proved fruitless. Nobody wanted to tell him anything, all clearly fearing that only trouble could come, either in the form of higher taxes or who knew what, from two officials and a foreigner walking about across their fields. Everybody said the same thing: 'I don't know.' They saw nothing, knew nothing, denied everything. That, at least, was clear.

Now, however, as he enjoyed the fine food and stimulating company of this little lunch party, Bleuchamps reflected that this was more like it. One of the other guests was a renowned professor of geology by the name of Dr Nagy—though Bleuchamps pronounced it 'Nagi' rather than 'Nudge' as a local would—who was highly esteemed not just in Europe but around the world. Surely, thought Major Bleuchamps, this man could tell him all he needed to know; but would he be willing to?

The food was delicious and the strong wines were of an old vintage. Conversation proceeded in fluent English, and Major Bleuchamps began at last to feel at home. After the depressing experience of those days spent walking fruitlessly back and forth across a bleak, muddy bog, he at last found himself in an oasis of civilisation. Stretching his long legs beneath the table, he sat back in his chair. Yes, this was more like it.

He glanced around in inconspicuous, British fashion. The white walls were almost entirely concealed behind copperplate engravings in antique frames, and two tall, narrow serving tables ran along the whole wall facing the windows. The dining room chairs were all in the same style: a subdued shade of green with pleasantly faded gilding. The young major, who had seen much good furniture at the homes of his relatives, inwardly dated the ensemble to the late eighteenth century. In one corner was a round, white ceramic stove from the same period; he had seen something similar in Schönbrunn, while passing through Vienna.

In the middle of the table stood three large silver goblets, in each of which a few yellow roses were already beginning to wilt. Now and then a drooping petal fell noiselessly onto the tablecloth.

The shuffling butler moved around the room, serving grapes and little yellow apples known as Ananas reinettes.

'Major Bleuchamps, you really must try the apples; I don't believe you'll find tastier ones anywhere else in the world.'

The woman who spoke was sitting next to the host and in front of the window; lit from behind, her face was entirely shadowed, but he could see that she was no longer young. The bright sunlight shone through her crown of black hair, and a band of grey ran like a vein of silver through her curls. A few strands of hair had freed themselves from their pins, and in the sunlight they glowed about her head like a halo. She was smiling at him, her expression almost motherly. Her face was still in shadow, and he could only see her eyes clearly. They were ever-so-slightly protuberant, and of a most unusual colour: a yellowish grey, like onyx. Her mouth was serious, but a smile danced around those eyes…

Bleuchamps trusted her at once. He did not know her name—they had been introduced, of course, but these foreign names were so peculiar—and he remembered only that she was Countess something-or-other.

'Thank you, Your Ladyship,' he said, then explained that he had been sent from Britain in search of oil. It had so far been, he confessed, a fruitless endeavour, and the officials he had spoken to had been of no help. It was, however, of enormous importance to him and he would be grateful for any assistance. Perhaps Her Ladyship would be so good as to ask 'Professor Nagi' if he might give him some information… Being an Englishman, Bleuchamps naturally framed the request in a slightly more diffident manner: 'It really would be splendid if…'

'Certainly,' replied the onyx-eyed woman. 'We shall arrange that at once.'

Turning to the professor, she spoke a few words in a language Bleuchamps did not understand. The professor adjusted the gold-rimmed spectacles at the end of his long nose with what was clearly a habitual gesture, then turned to Bleuchamps and invited him to visit him at home, where he would show him all the relevant maps.

'Today is Sunday, so I have no other engagements. Feel free to drop by any time this afternoon.'

A famously terse man, he turned away, having said all he meant to say.

'And afterwards, if you still have time, do join us at the theatre,' said another woman, who sat at the far end of the table near the host. 'Then at least you can say that you had one full day. You won't understand the language, of course, but it's Shakespeare, so perhaps you'll be able to follow the plot? You and the Consul are both welcome to join me in my box; I hope seeing Shakespeare in another language will prove an interesting experience!'

Trying not to show his astonishment, Bleuchamps glanced at Mr Miller, who replied at once.

'Awfully generous of you, we'd be delighted; the later the night ends the better as far as my friend is concerned: a car will be taking him to catch the Orient Express.'

The butler threw open the double doors; coffee would be served in the salon. The guests were shown into a rather cluttered room which gave the impression of having a little too much of everything. The walls were crowded with portraits from a variety of different historical periods; there were large and small oil paintings, watercolours of ladies in Biedermeier costume, and a plethora of framed miniatures. There must have been at least seven clocks, all beautiful, of bronze or wood, on top of cupboards, on the mantelpiece or on the walls. Inlaid or solid silver boxes stood piled on top of each other on the tables and there were larger chests on the floor. It was also surprising to see that in contrast to the elegant furniture, a wide, bed-like divan occupied one corner. This all seemed rather outlandish to Bleuchamps, who inwardly ascribed the room's appearance to 'Eastern influences'.

All were seated, and the smell of coffee mingled with cigarette smoke as they talked of this and that. Leaning forward in his chair, the Calvinist archdeacon told them that a charity bazaar was once again being organised, just like in the old days, to raise money for the orphanage. It could not, of course, be held in the city dance hall; the municipal authorities would not host such an event. Instead it would be held in the orphanage itself, with the school benches pushed against the walls to create enough space.

'We'll borrow a rug for the floor. And if the ladies were willing to take care of the stalls and…well, perhaps the refreshments too…I mean to say, I'm sure we can count on your assistance. Those are the most important things, and then the day will be a tremendous success!'

Bleuchamps was not particularly interested in any of this, but nodded approvingly when he saw the ladies and the Consul do likewise. He sat a little behind the archdeacon, who was still leaning forward in his chair, and Bleuchamps found his eye drawn to the man's coat. It was much too large, as though it had been tailored for some altogether plumper archdeacon in more affluent times. Now it sat rumpled upon his slender frame, and the Major suddenly understood that this was a picture of concealed poverty: the poor man could not properly feed himself and his one frock coat was shiny from years of wear.

The guests said goodbye, and everyone set off home. Bleuchamps had the impression that there was something slightly overdone—slightly theatrical—in the way the hosts were thanked for their hospitality. It was only a passing impression, however, and at the time he thought nothing of it. On the stairs, the onyx-eyed woman looked over her shoulder.

'When do you set off?'

'One in the morning,' the Consul answered for him. 'Not even worth going to bed.'

'In that case,' she said, 'come and see me for a cup of tea after the theatre. That will pass the time until your departure.'

Bleuchamps left with Professor Nagy, and they drove down winding streets between low buildings until at last they came to a one-storey house across the road from the university grounds. From inside, the imposing structure of the Geographical Institute could be clearly seen; its tall windows reflected late-afternoon sunlight into the professor's humble dwelling, so that from here the building appeared like a giant precision instrument, the mute and perfect embodiment of a noble aim. Major Bleuchamps looked across the street with interest, and Professor Nagy spoke for the first time since they set off together.

'Expressive piece of architecture, isn't it? Even from a distance you can see that it serves a scientific purpose. I consider it a perfect example of its type, constructed on very thorough practical and scientific principles. Back then...'

In the professor's eye there gleamed something like love and fatherly pride, then he turned away.

'Please sit down, Major,' he said, gesturing to the room's only chair.

Aside from having only one chair, the room was also strange in several other respects. In one corner stood a bed, and beside it a washstand. The one chair was made of pine, as was the single large table. There was no other furniture, and in any case there would hardly have been space for more, since one whole side of the room was taken up by a great mass of books. Books upon books upon books, stacked in great columns that rose towards the ceiling, alongside sheaves of documents and rolled maps in canvas bindings. Everything was stacked high, but in perfect order: from every sheaf of documents or bundle of maps there protruded a little tongue, upon each of which had been pencilled a reference comprising several letters or numbers.

'You're interested in the oil fields, aren't you? The relevant details are all here,' said the professor, running a practised finger along the protruding paper tongues until he came to a particularly thick bundle of papers.

'It's a good thing I keep these here with me, and not over there,' he said, jutting his long, bespectacled nose towards the Geographical Institute. 'They'd never let you get your hands on them; everything's been reclassified as a "state secret".'

He gave a quiet, sardonic laugh, and placed the bundle on the table in front of Major Bleuchamps. The young man wished to rise and give the professor his chair, but the older man waved the offer away.

'No, no, sit down. During my teaching days I got used to standing and giving lessons to people sitting down. Now, let's get to work.'

Professor Nagy spoke with remarkable clarity. First he gave a broad overview of the region's geology, outlining the synclinal and antiformal synclinal structures, igneous cupolas and other invisible wrinkles hidden beneath the earth's surface, though detectable by gravitational or magnetic methods. He then went on to describe his own techniques, honed through years of study in remote parts of the world. One by one he unfurled a series of maps, the first giving a general overview of the region, followed by several showing the precise geological contours of a given area. Then there were geological cross-sections, and even diagrams of individual boreholes.

He spoke for a long time, and in all his life Bleuchamps had never heard such complex matters explained so clearly. It was dark by the time the professor finished, but at last he rolled up some maps and geological diagrams and handed them to Bleuchamps.

'These are duplicates. You can take them, and I personally vouch for their reliability.'

The young Englishman was astounded at the professor's generosity. That he should unconditionally hand over documents answering every possible geological question... What he had given him was worth a fortune! Millions of pounds! And he was willing simply to hand it all over, to a complete stranger? There was something, he suspected, that he was not being told, and the feeling made him uneasy. At last he felt compelled to voice his disquiet.

'Tell me, sir, why are you willing to give all this to me, just like that? You must know, after all, what these are worth?'

'Of course I do! I'm giving them to you quite deliberately. Quite deliberately. You remember the Countess, at lunch today? She told me to give you everything you needed, and so I'm giving it to you.'

'The lady who sat next to the host?'

The professor gave an almost imperceptible smile:

'Yes, next to the host. We do that when...'

He checked himself, and almost angrily changed the subject.

'In any case, I'll give documents to whomever I please! It's no business of anyone else's! This'—he gestured at the bundle of documents—'is my property, you understand? I'll do with it as I please!'

Bleuchamps stood up, regretting that he seemed to have stumbled inadvertently into some personal matter which was no business of his. He had strayed, in other words, from that wisest and most quintessentially English rule of propriety whereby it is forbidden to ask any other human being, least of all one's closest friend, any personal question whatsoever. Adopting his habitual mask of cool inscrutability, he tucked the bundle of documents under his arm and bade his host a brisk, business-like good day.

'I shall inform my company that we are in your debt,' he said with a slight bow.

The professor escorted him to the Rolls-Royce, which was waiting in front of the house, and stood motionless as it purred off into the dark.

Bleuchamps, feeling suddenly guilty that he had not been more profuse in his thanks, looked back through the rear window. The professor was still standing on the pavement, but not looking at the departing vehicle. Instead he was gazing straight ahead, through the fence-posts of the university garden, towards the high windows of the Geographical Institute. His head was raised in stubborn, bitter defiance.

The car drove first to the British Consulate, where Bleuchamps quickly packed away his newly acquired treasure, then changed into evening dress with equal haste. A few minutes later he and Mr Miller set off.

'To the Hungarian theatre,' Mr Miller said to the driver.

The car set off, driving very slowly on account of the appalling road surface—nothing but potholes—and the

Rolls-Royce's decidedly delicate chassis. The driver snaked down the street, sometimes close up against the left-hand pavement and sometimes to the right, trying all the while to avoid the deep, muddy puddles which pitted the asphalt. Even so, now and then he miscalculated, and the car made a sickening crunch as it lurched through a pothole.

They drove out onto the town's main square, which was just as dilapidated as the preceding street. Huge arc lights mercilessly illuminated the huge potholes and lakes of mud.

Here too it was possible to drive only very slowly. Along both pavements a great throng of people paraded beneath electric street-lamps more blinding than any daylight. All were dressed in their finery, with the women in peony-bright skirts and unbelievably high heels. They had rouged lips and their eyes were outlined in dusky black. Beside them walked pink-cheeked officers in jaunty uniforms, gold-braided caps on their heads and swords clanking at their hips. Big spurs rang on the cobblestones, and they strode with a manly, purposeful swagger.

There was a strange contrast between this noisy parade of bright, colourful people in silk and velvet, and the sober façades of the respectable burghers' houses lining the square. It seemed to Bleuchamps that he was witness to a very strange and remarkable sight, as though the characters and their background had been thrown together entirely at random, without any natural connection…

The Rolls-Royce turned suddenly, and they came face to face with a bronze statue depicting a seated man in a deeply pleated cloak. They passed behind it, and to Bleuchamps' eyes the man's head seemed much too small for the rest of the body. The patina seemed different, too, making the head seem somehow newer. Looking more closely, it was easy to see by the arc light's blinding glare that at the nape of the neck the cast did not quite meet: a hole yawned, as though at that point the casting bronze had run dry.

He wanted to ask what the meaning of this strange memorial could be, but the theatre was already approaching. It was a tasteful structure, with a high façade upheld on Doric columns and a roof that rose in a low pyramid.

Arc lights blazed here too, but the windows were dark, and the car turned into another street without stopping.

'This isn't where we're going?' asked Bleuchamps.

'No, that's the state theatre now. We're going to the Hungarian theatre, which is at the edge of the city. The very edge.'

They drove off down ever-darker streets.

'That was a very strange statue we drove past,' said Bleuchamps. 'The head seemed ridiculously small.'

'Oh, there's a story behind that. It used to be the statue of a Hungarian poet who was born here but the new town councillors decided to change the head and replace it with the bust of one of their leading politicians. The national foundry then stole most of the bronze, and that's how it turned out! Odd business, isn't it?'

They were still driving extremely slowly. The arc lights were behind them now, as were all the tall buildings. Now there were only single-storey houses interspersed with large orchards. Here and there they caught the glimmer of a solitary light bulb.

At last they came to a large, empty plot, with a few wooden posts attesting to some desultory effort to fence the space off. They turned in. At the back of this plot stood a large and very odd-looking building: Major Bleuchamps had never seen a theatre like it. A high building with a split-level roof was outlined against the sky, and as the car circled the structure he realised that it comprised four equal wings, each with a monstrously oversized entranceway. They stopped by the second such wing, and at the bottom of the enormous doorway a much smaller door opened. This was the public entrance.

A man in theatrical costume had evidently been waiting for them. He did not speak, but merely gestured that they should follow him. Passing through the curtained doorway, Bleuchamps found himself already facing the stage. The performance had already begun and the lights were so blinding that he sensed rather than saw the audience in the space beyond, but the actor was already leading them to one side and up two wooden steps. This was the box. Bleuchamps greeted the ladies and sat down.

'It's *The Comedy of Errors*,' whispered the lady who had invited him.

Mr Miller and Mr Bleuchamps looked at one another. Both had been members of the Oxford University Dramatic Society in their student days, where this wildest of Shakespeare's comedies was a perennial favourite. Even now, both knew the play almost by heart.

'Very interesting,' said Major Bleuchamps, turning to the stage with renewed attention.

The play is fabulous burlesque and so utterly improbable that were it not for the playwright's consummate skill, a modern audience would never enjoy it. The actors made very inventive use of a stage barely six metres wide.

They performed before a featureless, blue-grey background, intended perhaps to suggest an endless vista of sky, or fog rising above a tranquil sea, while a single-arched bridge stood as sole prop in the middle of the stage. Two large sheets of yellow cloth hung at either side of the stage to represent two houses, and from each a few steps led up towards the bridge. A few benches, painted white to suggest marble columns, stood upright against the stage backdrop.

The burlesque unfurled in front of the grey sky, on the bridge, on the steps, and in front of the marble columns, the actors constantly moving about the stage. The effect of these figures leaping and capering before a peaceful grey background irresistibly brought to mind the Renaissance paintings of Palma Vecchio, though the costumes had all been made from the cheapest peasant cloth.

The actors delivered their lines in a quick, cheerful patter, moving around the stage with contagious good humour. It was as though everything were nothing but one big joke, which of course in the case of this particular play is quite true, and the spectators forgot the absurdities of the plot as the action sped dizzyingly along and the characters continually swapped roles.

When the curtain fell at the end of the first act the footlights were illuminated, though these were so few and gave such feeble light that they scarcely made any difference.

The building had been constructed on a cross-shape design, with four wings of equal length. Between the walls and the central hall were many thick pillars of old stone holding up an unpainted ceiling. It was clear that the structure had originally been intended for some other purpose, and that boxes had subsequently been constructed in the gaps between the pillars. Rows of benches filled the central space, all facing the stage which had been built into one of the four radial axes. Another, as we have seen, formed the entrance, and the remaining two were used as cloakrooms. At the end of each of these were the same grotesquely oversized doors with wicket gates at their base, through which people came and went.

Bleuchamps looked around, bemused.

'I've never seen such a theatre in my life,' he said.

'Neither has anybody else, I should imagine,' laughed the plump, grey-haired woman who had invited them. 'Do you know what this building used to be? A barn.'

'A barn?'

'Yes. It was built by the Calvinist church in 1792. There's still a plaque outside. Down there where the seats are is where they used to thresh the grain, back before there were steam threshers, and each thresher needed a lot of space to work. That's why the four wings all have such enormous doors; carts piled high with wheat used to ride straight in here. Behind the stage is another door just like the others. When they invented steam threshers, this space was converted into a granary. Now, with their lands all appropriated by the state, the church doesn't need a granary, so the Hungarian Theatre Society moved here when they were expelled from the city theatre.

The old lady spoke dispassionately, as though all this were the most natural thing in the world, but some deeper emotion burned in her eyes.

'And you see this upholstery here in the boxes?' Mr Miller whispered, running a hand along the back of a chair. 'Do you know what this is? It's the material from all the city's Hungarian flags. The chairs here in the boxes, and the benches down there, are upholstered in the red part, while the green went to make the curtains.'

Bleuchamps glanced around once more. The whole hall was packed, with not a single free space on the benches, and at least four or five people in every box. All except one, directly beside the stage, in which a heavy-set man with a black beard sat alone. He was plainly too hot, and sat distractedly twisting a lock of his beard around a plump, stubby finger. Mr Miller noticed Major Bleuchamps looking at the man.

'Ah, that's the chief of police,' he said. 'He has to sit through every Hungarian theatre production, from the moment the curtain rises to the moment it falls. The poor man must be bored out of his wits!'

At that moment the curtain rose and the faint lights in the auditorium went out. Shakespeare's delightful nonsense began once more against the same featureless backdrop.

The play ended, and the same actor escorted the two English gentlemen through a side-door.

'You'll get out quicker this way,' he smiled.

Bleuchamps felt impelled to express the pleasure this strange performance had given him, and the artistic merit it displayed. He wished to say that he respected—even admired—the spirit of perseverance which sustained an enterprise of this sort even in the hardest of times. He struggled, alas, to find a suitable German expression, and in desperation simply repeated some trite banality in English as the young actor wrung him by the hand.

'Very nice. Very nice. Really very nice…'

They drove off once more into the dark streets, the pools of mud glinting in the beam of the powerful headlights. They passed the main square, then more dark streets, until at last they reached their destination.

Water simmered in a big copper samovar, while the embers beneath it cast a cheery red glow about the room. The tall lady with the white streak in her hair and her two younger sisters were serving tea and sandwiches, and hot, savoury pastries from a silver serving dish.

'It's always good to have something warm to eat before a journey,' said the Countess.

Bleuchamps was stretched out on a big divan which seemed to be the room's main article of furniture, and had begun to feel pleasantly drowsy.

The shaded lamps, the high, arched ceiling—and perhaps this little late-night feast as well, for he was not a man given to restraint when food was offered—had all conspired to fill him with a sense of ease and well-being; the place felt so homely.

One of the girls played soft preludes on the piano, while the Consul leaned on the lid and chatted with the other.

Their hostess, meanwhile, sat on the divan next to Bleuchamps, a slim hand resting on her knee. The young major felt so at ease in her presence that it occurred to him he might ask her about the documents. How could it be that the professor had so generously handed over such a valuable prize?

It was if she had read his thoughts. Fixing him with that onyx gaze, she asked, 'Professor Nagy gave you all the information you needed?'

'He did, yes. It was rather a surprise, actually, since it's worth an absolute fortune, and simply to hand it over unconditionally, without any recompense whatsoever... A fellow might have been forgiven for wondering if everything was really quite as it seemed, were it not for the absolute confidence he inspires.'

'Oh, you don't need to worry about that. I can assure you that everything you received is quite reliable and factually sound.'

Bleuchamps hesitated for a moment, then, steeling himself, asked what was on his mind.

'The professor said that he only did it, gave them to me I mean, because Your Ladyship...'

'Oh, that's just because he knows I only recommend people I know can be taken seriously. You're from Anglo-Persian.'

The lady now turned her whole body to face him, and the streak in her hair glowed silver in the lamplight.

'That's why? Just because I'm from Anglo-Persian?'

She smiled. 'Yes, that's why.' Eyes smiling, she went on,

'That's precisely the reason. You see, Major Bleuchamps, we would like your nation to develop financial interests in this country'—she corrected herself—'in this part of the country. We want you to come here, and we want you to have an incentive to come here. Ideally you should have very large financial interests in this part of the world.'

'But why?' asked Bleuchamps.

'Because the British simply aren't interested in this little corner of Europe. What interest you are business opportunities, and petroleum is a big business, perhaps the biggest. That's why you'll come. And if you come, you'll see what's really here.'

'In the ground?'

The Countess gave another soft smile.

'Yes, in the ground... And above it, too.'

It was the middle of the night when Major Bleuchamps left the city. The Consul accompanied him.

'It's better if I take you,' said Mr Miller. 'Otherwise it's just endless checkpoints and searches.'

They set off at two in the morning, hoping to make the Orient Express, which would was due at a nearby station at six. The place was only about forty miles away but the roads were so bad that there was nowhere the car could pick up any sort of speed. The eighty-horsepower Rolls-Royce purred down a wide country road which had not been paved for many years. The car's bodywork was jet-black, polished to a mirror sheen, while the two large headlights and the engine casing were chrome nickel. The overall impression was of some strange, fairy-tale animal with a silver nose and eyes.

The Union Jack fluttered on the bonnet and the two English gentlemen reclined in the plush-upholstered interior. Perhaps now and then they dozed off.

They were heading uphill, and the driver was pleasantly surprised to find that the road conditions up here were much better; this country road saw little traffic, so in places it was in almost perfect condition. He shifted up into third—a rare occurrence indeed—and stepped on the accelerator: the powerful motor roared up the incline as though eating up the pale band of road before it.

The trouble happened at the crest: the car crunched over two large bumps and the engine began rattling wildly. The driver braked and the car came to a halt.

'What happened?' asked the Consul.

By way of response, the driver uttered one of those marvellously long and convoluted English curses which in the literature of that country are generally elided under the term 'profanity'.

This was clearly a major breakdown.

'Can you fix it?' asked Bleuchamps.

The driver's reply came to him from behind the car's

upraised bonnet. 'Three quarters of an hour, sir.'

'Can we help?' asked the Consul.

'No, thank you sir.'

The first glimmers of dawn showed in the eastern sky. The two men walked up and down beside the car for a time, then sat down on the hillside. For a few minutes they were silent, and as Bleuchamps looked at that dim glow on the eastern horizon, his mind ran over the experiences of the past few days. He thought of his days spent tramping through sodden fields, of the documents which the professor had given him, and of all his strange experiences the day before. He turned to Mr Miller.

'You know, I really had a wonderful time yesterday afternoon. It reminded me of coming home after a long, hard, dirty trek and taking a hot bath, but in this case a cultural bath. You've got a marvellous little society here.'

'The people you met yesterday are even more interesting than you imagine, and there's a lot here which is not at all as it may seem at first glance.'

The Consul thought for a moment, then went on.

'Take our lunch yesterday, for instance. Our host, as I said on our way over, is the head of the Hungarian parliamentary party. Still, you shouldn't imagine that the house is actually his.'

'What? Whose is it, then?'

'It belongs to a very old aristocratic lady. Now if they're

entertaining strangers they always invite them there, since it's the only grand dining room in the city which is still in the hands of its previous occupant. The others have all been "requisitioned", which means that every house is full of newcomers. The former inhabitants, even the grandest, have at most a single bedroom left to themselves. Everything else has been taken away by the authorities, so if they want to host a lunch or dinner they have to host it in the last dining room owned by a Hungarian. The actual owner, the elderly lady I mentioned, doesn't attend such events, but goes to stay with some relative or other.'

'How interesting,' said Bleuchamps, and both were silent for a moment. Then Mr Miller went on.

'The fact is, it's a marvel they can even scrape together enough food to host a luncheon like that, though not so long ago they were all well-off people. Now they barely have a crust to live on, and everybody has to chip in to finance a dinner party. Still, the gentleman and lady at the two ends of the table play the munificent host and hostess, and the others play the guests. But I'm the only one who has realised this—and I pretend I haven't cottoned on.'

Big clouds drifted across the inky sky and the band of light along the eastern horizon grew brighter.

'They also borrow the table decorations from one another; I've seen those goblets in plenty of other apartments. They still want everything to look tasteful.'

'The dining room was perfectly arranged for the purpose,' said Bleuchamps, 'but the salon seemed a touch cluttered.'

'That's because any article of value was put there after the authorities confiscated all but those two rooms. Every painting, clock, ornament or other precious knick-knack. It's true! Didn't you notice that every room we've been in has had some sort of ottoman or divan in the corner? That's where its occupant sleeps, though when guests come they pretend it's just a sofa. That's the thing about these people: they're desperate not to show the miserable condition of their lives. I have no doubt that the cost of the theatre box is also paid by joint subscription, at least when they're entertaining a foreign visitor. They split it among themselves.'

Miller fell silent for a moment, then added, as a sort of afterthought, 'The whole thing must take an ungodly amount of energy...'

Again there was a pause, and neither spoke. The first bright ray of sunlight at last rose above the distant hills, illuminating the whole landscape.

'And then take that professor you met. He's a very great man, absolutely one of the best in his field, and I dare say he could make a great deal of money teaching in Britain or America. But he doesn't want to go. They kicked him out of the university, expelled him from the Geographical Institute, and now he lives opposite the very building he helped design a decade ago. It was one of the most advanced earth science institutes in the world back then, with all the most up-to-date equipment. So there he remains, right across the street, keeping an eye on it, so to speak. But you saw that yourself, I'm sure. In any case, he now makes a living as foreman at a brick factory, and was only able to receive you at home in the afternoon because it was a Sunday. During the week he works all day.

'They're certainly a very particular group of people,' said Bleuchamps, and he remembered the woman with the streak of white in her black hair. Picturing her, he could still see those gleaming onyx eyes.

'And the lady we visited last night?'

'She's the cousin of the leader of the Hungarian Party. She's a widow and her two sons were killed in the war. She doesn't have anybody now, but perhaps she's the strongest of all…'

He fell silent again. Bleuchamps waited for him to resume, but he said no more.

It was bright daylight now, and a broad hem of gold now fringed the horizon. A flock of blue-tinted cumulus clouds drifted unhurriedly across the rolling landscape, and far off in the distance the violet bulk of a single, volcano-like mountain rose out of the haze.

'The car's all right now, sir,' said the driver.

Mr Miller stood up, his pale blue eyes fixed on some far-distant point. He was not looking at the rocky hillside, but perhaps at the far horizon, or towards those invisible ranges which reared high into the clouds. Placing one of his big feet on the car's running board, he looked back at Major Bleuchamps.

'That's the main thing, old boy: never lose hope.'

HELEN IN SPARTA

Rosy-fingered dawn had only just begun to rend the veil of night when a swift young messenger appeared in the streets of Sparta, calling through the doorways of the sturdy houses. He called out to the old men of the city, to the solemn, bearded patriarchs, to the heroes and warriors, and to the shepherds who tended the cattle of the gods. All were invited to the palace of the Spartan king, spear-famed Menelaus, son of Atreus, for a feast to celebrate the tenth anniversary of his return from Troy.

The guests made their way up towards the citadel, the acropolis, in a long double file. They flowed through the echoing gateway, built by cyclopes from huge blocks of undressed stone, then passed before the shrine to ox-eyed Hera. Entering the throne room, the royal megaron, they sat down around the marble hearth in the centre of the colonnaded hall.

The king himself sat across from them, sprawled across the hall's highest chair. This was a wide-footed bronze throne, and substantial though it was, the king's great bulk filled it entirely. His fine purple cloak strained against his swollen paunch like a ship's canvas sail, rippling and bellying in a favourable wind. He had grown heavy since his return from Troy, and both his hair and ruddy, spade-shaped beard were greying.

This was the feast day, when every man would receive his just portion. Menelaus himself grilled sizzling, fatty strips of pork, both belly and rump, over the open fire, and handed these unctuous prizes to his guests. All drank of the sweet, heady Cyprus wine, into which servants had grated ewe's cheese and sifted white flour as an added delight.

When all had eaten and drunk their fill—with, as befitted such a feast, much loud smacking of lips, but no conversation—the bard was summoned.

He stepped out from among the guests, took his place by an alabaster column, and began to sing. And of what should the bard of gods and heroes sing, if not the siege of Troy? That great struggle was the subject of a thousand tales, recounted by those lucky enough to have avoided the grim fate which stalks all fighting men. They who, by the grace of the immortals, had not bitten the bitter earth and had returned alive from man-devouring battle. In those days all wandering bards sang the tales of Troy.

And his winged words soared.

Much was already familiar to his listeners, for these deeds had been sung from house to house by lesser bards.

Everybody knew the tale, and only through apter or more vivid metaphors, or some more luminous recitation, could one poet shine above his peers.

The bard was singing of the death of Paris, when Philoctetes shoots this wicked seducer with a poisoned arrow. The audience was delighted. They were laughing and whooping, some even stamping their feet in approval, when a figure appeared in the doorway of the gynaikon, or women's quarters.

Helen.

Everybody turned and fell silent. Even the bard.

The goddess-like queen advanced slowly, with measured, even tread. She glided towards them, as light as the lightest scrap of foam which floats upon a calm ocean, and as she crossed the stone-flagged megaron her feet made no more sound than the paws of a lioness, stalking yellow-eyed and alone amid the dewy grass. Or like a white cloud on a languid summer's day, drifting across a sky of purest azure. That was how pale-armed Helen entered the hall.

All the men in the hall, both young and old, at once fell to whispering.

'Worth fighting a hundred battles, worth dying a hundred deaths for such a woman!'

She was no longer young; that famous golden hair was streaked with grey and there were lines around her sea-blue eyes; but she was still magnificent. Her lips were still as full and rosy as a kiss, her smile still the captivating smile of a goddess.

A violet veil floated about her slender form as she advanced, catching now and then the outline of a leg, swirling about her like the eternal gaze of male desire.

She came in and sat down on the ivory throne to Menelaus' left. She seemed to slip a little deeper into her veil as she sat down, as when little birds bury themselves in a ruffled mass of feathers. Then, with queenly calm, she gazed around the room.

The king gestured to the bard, who began again to sing. He sang of how Paris' legs buckled, and he fell with hands splayed in the dirt. In merciless detail he related the spasms wracking that godlike body, the black blood springing from his open mouth, the awful rattle, and every other torment of a man succumbing to a painful death. Many watched the queen's face as she listened, but none saw any change in her calm smile.

When the bard paused, another old soldier from the Siege of Troy, a man by the name of Thersites, rose and turned to Menelaus.

'Truly, noble king, the gods have never bestowed undue favour upon you! Why did they not grant you the honour of killing this worthless seducer yourself?'

Menelaus looked up, anger in his eyes; he well remembered Thersites, wickedest among the Achaeans, and his constant goading taunts during the siege. Menelaus despised him, but also feared his quick wit.

'Snake-tongued man, you have never spoken more truly! The gods never bestowed much favour upon me, but heaped my back with worry and care! Golden Aphrodite even gave away my own wife as a gift to another man! My own wife!'

He turned sharply towards Helen.

'How could you run off with such a worm?'

'Aphrodite clouded my thoughts,' Helen replied with the same calm smile.

His anger building, the king continued.

'Run off with a runt like that and leave me, the equal to any hero of old! All the other Achaeans—Diomedes, Ajax, Odysseus—they all had some immortal on their side, helping them in battle: one with a suit of impenetrable armour, another with a bright flame, still another with a terrible roar. I alone had to fight my battles without divine help!'

The king looked around for approbation, but the crowd remained silent. He went on, more hotly than ever.

'Everyone knows it! When mighty Hector strode the field, challenging any man to single combat, I alone stepped forth like the red-eyed, battle-ready bull. All those famous heroes? They sat on their hands, while I, Menelaus, sprang forth like the big-hearted boar cornered in a thicket, ready to tear the hunter in two with sharp-scything tusks! That is how I leapt at Hector.'

Thersites shrugged.

'Not that you actually fought him, of course.'

'Agamemnon forbade it! That too, I expect, was the work of some malicious deity whispering in his ear. Though the foam-mouthed stallion rears and strains, and stamps his hooves in the dirt, still he is held by a good harness. So I stepped back from the fray, though it went against the wishes of my warrior's heart. Agamemnon was the commander, do you understand? I had no choice! Do you know the highest virtue in war? Discipline!'

He looked around again, but still nobody spoke. Turning on Thersites, he vented his fury.

'Worthless, dog-hearted man! Why did I not kill Paris? You ask me that, when you were there and saw the fight? The whole army saw! Even the women of Troy saw, watching from their high walls! First, though he was white with dread, he threw his spear at me. Then I threw mine, and it flew with such force that it burst his shield, shearing clean through both armour and woollen tunic. The worm would have tasted black death then and there were it not for his cursed nimbleness; he twisted his slender body aside and dodged the spearpoint. Then I sprang upon him with my sword, but it broke on his armour and left him unwounded! That's when I grabbed him with my two strong hands, taking him by the horsehair plume of his helmet and dragging him back towards our lines, as the lion clamps the goat-kid by the head and drags it back towards his den! But what happened then? The chinstrap broke, leaving me standing there like a fool with nothing but the helmet in my hand!'

'And then Paris vanished,' laughed Thersites, with a sly sideways glance at Helen.

Menelaus also turned to her.

'You saw it too, didn't you? You were there on the wall?'

'I saw,' replied the goddess-like woman, the smile never fading from her lips.

'And you saw how pale the coward was? And how he trembled?'

'I saw that too.'

'He always tried to avoid the real man's fighting, the hand-to-hand combat. I remember he usually wore no armour, just a leopard-skin cloak, and preferred to shoot arrows from a distance. The bow is the coward's weapon, and that's what he was! A coward!'

'Yes,' Helen said softly. 'He was a coward, that's true.' She paused for a moment, then sighed. 'I despised him for it.'

'Ah? Despised? That's a good word. But tell me, did you see our single combat? Were you really there on the walls? Did you see our life-and-death struggle? This is something I have never asked before, but I ask it now!' The king raised his great bulk into a more upright position and looked at her excitedly. 'Tell me, who did you want to win that day? Me or Paris? Tell me truly, me or Paris?'

Absolute silence fell upon the hall, the guests hardly daring to breathe. Sensing that a moment of high drama had arrived, every eye turned to that sublime woman behind her translucent veil. Alone upon that ivory throne, she sat in marmoreal calm. Her blue eyes opened no wider, her smile showed no less serene, and no trace of a frown puckered that snow-white brow. When her answer came it was silvery and clear, neither louder nor softer than before.

'I wished victory for you, Lord Menelaus.'

A relieved murmur of approbation rippled through the hall, and the king sat back in his throne with a triumphant laugh.

'That's good! I like that! That's good!'

He repeated this several times, amid bouts of laughter. In his pleasure he kept clapping his fat thighs together, as though crushing flies between his knees. His great belly shook, sending ripples across the purple fabric of his cloak like waves across a wind-ruffled bay. At last the laughter subsided enough for him to speak.

'Wine! Wine! A cup of my best wine!'

A cup was hurriedly fetched, and he drained it. Thick gobbets of grease and wine speckled his beard and gaping mouth as he roared, 'Let that be a lesson. There is no glory for cowards, nor any hiding place either! Now, bard, sing of me! Sing of my deeds! You'll be richly rewarded if you do well!'

The bard began to sing of how the king guarded the body of Patroclus against the swarming Trojans. Bound by tradition, however, he felt obliged to sing too that the king was at length driven back by superior numbers, and that Telamonian Ajax then cut a path through them to retrieve the body.

The King of Sparta flew once more into a terrible rage, and violently cursed the bard. It made no difference that his song had used the most beautiful adjectives to describe his person, and the most evocative metaphors for his ferocious and magnificent deeds.

'No! Not like that! Lies!'

The king began his own account, telling his assembled listeners how this or that event had truly happened. The guests, grateful for the wine and food, applauded his vituperative curses. Menelaus went on, with much boasting, to tell them how many men he had slain, and how little mercy he had shown them. He praised his own strength, heroism and audacity, the words tumbling from him amid a storm of wild gestures.

'I had him like this, his legs kicking, then I crushed his skull with a single blow, like this…'

He went on for a very long time, and as dusk began to fall they brought in lighted torches. Menelaus, however, showed no sign of fatigue, and the unbroken stream of bombast, embellishment and outright lies still flowed. Unnoticed,

Helen rose and walked with her long stride from the wine-heavy hall.

Outside the sun had just set. She stopped in the doorway and took a deep breath of the fresh evening air. Then she walked towards the edge of the sheer palace walls, and rested lily-white fingertips on the lip of the parapet. She stood there for a long time, gazing far, far off into the distance.

Dusk filled the valley below with a copper gauze of mist, and only the summit of the Taygetus on the valley's far side still caught the last, red light of day. Here and there in the shadowed depths a glint of reflected sunlight still flickered in the fast-flowing waters of the Eurotas, and a handful of lonely stars twinkled in the steel-green sky. Dust clouds raised by tramping feet still lingered over the valley, obscuring the trail up to the acropolis. A few throaty horn calls broke the twilit stillness: shepherds and cowherds driving their animals down from upland pastures.

And Helen remembered the past. Those many evenings—how many!—spent on another city's ramparts.

Mount Ida had glowed just the same, catching the sunset, and the snaking waters of the Scamander had reflected its dying light with the same bright flashes of gold. Then, too, the dust had risen from tramping feet, and horns had sounded in the dark, but those had been the horns of heroes calling to one another, great men who did battle for her sake across ten long years…

How many thousands had died for her beauty?

And on those walls of Troy, a dark-eyed youth in a leopard-skin cloak would come to stand beside her. Her lover, Paris, the man whose name she had just publicly scorned.

He used to come to her on the ramparts, padding on silent feet like a big cat. They would embrace, his hands caressing her back, his body warm like the furs he wore, and she could feel in his whole being a great ache of desire. His mouth, hot like fire, would kiss her, bite her neck, his hands pinioning her arms, moving across her body, pressing into her flesh…

Wordlessly they would hold one another, above a battlefield strewn with bodies and a sinking sky. For a very long time. Until by degrees the summit of Mount Ida lost its glow, and the world beyond the walls disappeared.

Just like tonight.

Helen stood alone, watching the distant mountains fade to silhouettes, their outlines growing steadily less distinct until at last they vanished altogether. Like forgotten memories.

When darkness had consumed everything, fusing land and sky in a void of utter blankness, two big, slow tears formed in the corners of her eyes. They hesitated for a moment at her lashes, then trickled down exquisite cheeks to pool—two drops of purest crystal—in the folds of her violet veil.

TALKING NOTHING

In his later years—and perhaps his earlier years too—Prince Mihály Apafi of Transylvania[14] found affairs of state extremely tedious. He was obliged, however, to preside daily over long council sessions, where an assembly of 'learned gentlemen' taxed his ears with prolix advice. This was a great burden to him, especially since at that time his chancellor, Count Teleki, took care of all the routine business of state, leaving him to sit in restless boredom.

After these council meetings his advisors would stay for lunch, so that even over their food and drink the conversation was still of politics. When they at last departed, he would turn to his steward, Szentpáli.

'Come thou hither, Szentpáli my old friend, and let us talk nothing!'

What follows, then, is my own sort of 'talking nothing'. Short stories of no importance, and some not much shy of a hundred years old.

Little Jeannette

Both these stories concern Johanna Bethlen, or Countess Tholdalagi as she became. She was my grandfather's niece and everyone addressed her in French fashion as Jeannette. I knew her in her very old age, when she was stooped and wrinkled. In 1848, however, she was a young wife and exceptionally pretty. Her husband was a major in the Hungarian revolutionary army and Jeannette, deeply in love, followed the army wherever it went, in a carriage with glass windows.

In the autumn of 1849 they came at last to Világos, where the army laid down its arms and surrendered to the Russians. When Jeannette heard of the capitulation, she flew into a rage: despite her diminutive size no one could match the ferocity of her patriotism. She stormed into the main hall of the Bohus manor, which was crammed with Russian and Hungarian officers, and pushed her way through the crowd until she was face-to-face with General Görgey, the commander of the Hungarian forces[15]. Looking him straight in the eye, she addressed him in a voice as sharp and piercing as a whistle.

'Commander, you are a traitor!'

That was the fearless, resolute character of Jeannette Bethlen.

It is hardly surprising, then, that when her husband decided he really could not allow his fine, chased-silver French saddle pistols to fall into the hands of his captors, he entrusted them to his young wife.

'Hide these,' he said, 'and get them out.'

But where was she to put them? Where was the safest place, where nobody would look? At last she decided to sew them into the crinoline folds of her wide, hooped skirt.

The next day a long convoy of carriages set off from Világos, taking the women to Nagyvárad[16]. There were also a few Hungarian army officers who had disguised themselves as servants, coachmen and the like, to avoid Austrian or Russian captivity, but that is neither here nor there. The point, for our purposes, is that the convoy set off early in the morning, and they were advised not to stop anywhere on the way. It being August, however, the day was sure to be hot, the journey long—at least a hundred kilometres—and few sources of clean water were to be found in that part of the country. In addition to their standard provisions, therefore, the women were each given three or four watermelons as a tonic for thirst.

They set off, and all went well. They travelled unhindered, but still it was pitch dark by the time they reached the outskirts of Nagyvárad. Then, all of a sudden, the whole convoy drew to a halt. There were shouts from up ahead, and the swaying glow of a lantern.

'Gracious Heaven!' Jeannette thought in alarm. Gendarmes?'

This was plainly a search, which meant they were looking for either someone or something. Weapons, perhaps? What if they found the pistols in her skirts? That would be the end of her!

Already the lantern was approaching her carriage, and two silhouettes appeared at her window. Soldiers. From their gruff talk she could hear that they were Serbs or Croats, *Grenzers* from the southern borderlands.

'Do not abandon me Lord Jesus!' she whispered.

One man threw open the door and the other reached in with both hands, as though about to dive head-first into the carriage. He was reaching for her feet, under her skirts!

But there was no cause for alarm. The soldiers were not there to assault her, nor even to search her for weapons. What they wanted were the watermelons, which—there being nowhere else to put them—each woman had placed on the carriage floor by her feet. They found the one remaining watermelon and took it. Then, with an exultant chuckle, they slammed the door and moved on to the next carriage.

Thus did Mihály Tholdalagi's fine silver pistols arrive safely home, and so—after a little fright—did his young wife. And I heard this story from her own lips.

Lord, but what a long time ago all that was!

The Covered Bridge at Torda

Is there anyone who still remembers the covered bridge at Torda? Alas, it was torn down years ago and replaced with an iron bridge. But it was a beauty, without equal in the whole country. There was a similar bridge in Segesvár, of course, over the Küküllő, but the Torda bridge was longer, since the Aranyos is a broader river[17]. Or at least, it can be: at times the river dwindles to a trickle, then rises to a great flood, and so the riverbed, though often dry, is very broad.

The inhabitants of Torda were proud of their bridge. On the first pier facing the town, there was a sign which I myself saw many times:

'Pause, traveller, to behold this marvel of nature, and listen as the river murmurs its admiration.'

A pretty turn of phrase, and a deceptively modest one, for of course it was not really nature which formed the bridge, but the good joiners of Torda.

A toll was charged to use the bridge, and many a frugal carter chose to cross the Aranyos at the nearby ford instead. That was quite all right, but the town council worried that someone might get into difficulties trying to cross at the ford when the Aranyos was in spate. After much discussion they at last agreed to drive a short stake into the riverbed by the ford, and nail a sign to it:

'Warning! Do not cross if you cannot see this sign!'

That was the beneficent character of the Torda town council.

But it is not the point of this little story, which instead concerns what happened when word reached the council that a brewery which was then under construction on the far side of the bridge planned to transport a boiler from Kolozsvár. A huge boiler, perhaps forty hundredweight. When the town council heard of these plans, they immediately began to fret whether their precious bridge could bear such a load. A lengthy debate followed, and at last they decided to form a committee, composed of the foremost local experts, to assess the strength of the bridge.

The committee set off the next morning and began a thorough examination of the bridge. They tapped every beam and post and scrutinised every load-bearing point on the truss, down to the slenderest roof strut. Satisfied at last, they declared it their unanimous opinion that while the bridge was in outstanding condition, and might easily stand for another century, there was no question of it bearing such a tremendous weight, which was sure to make it buckle and collapse.

The toll warden stood in front of his box and watched in perplexity as the expert gentlemen prodded and sniffed his bridge, and even waded through the shallow water to stand underneath it. For the life of him he could not fathom what they were up to. Only when they had concluded their examination did they at last approach him.

'Listen here, my good fellow,' the committee chairman said. 'A boiler is on its way from Kolozsvár, and it's so heavy that it takes eight water buffalo to haul the wagon. We have established that such a weight would surely cause this bridge to collapse. As such, your strict orders are that under no circumstances whatsoever should it be allowed to cross. Be vigilant, because if you permit this boiler to cross and the bridge collapses, you will be held criminally liable! Do you understand?'

The toll warden frowned worriedly and scratched his head.

'There's a problem, sir.'

'A problem? What problem?'

'The thing is, sir, it already crossed this morning at dawn. What am I supposed to do now?'

An Oratorical Triumph

In the early 1880s, Archduke Karl Ludwig, the younger brother of Emperor Franz Joseph, was appointed honorary patron of every Red Cross institution in the Dual Monarchy. The president of the Red Cross in Hungary at that time was Gyula Károlyi, father of the future prime minister Mihály Károlyi[18]. He had become a relative of our family through his first marriage, though in fact he and my father had been good friends for many years before that. He recounted this story fresh from the oven, so to speak: after accompanying the Archduke as far as Kolozsvár, he came straight up to visit us at Bonchida.

He was a vivacious, lively man of excellent humour, and he told his tale with great gusto.

What happened was this: Archduke Karl Ludwig was on a tour of inspection of the Empire's Red Cross offices, and Gyula Károlyi accompanied him on the train from Budapest. Their first stop was Nagyvárad, and about halfway there, just after passing through Szolnok, the Archduke asked Károlyi to join him in his private carriage. The problem was that the Archduke had received a letter from Monsignor Schlauch, the bishop of Nagyvárad, which contained not only the very fine speech the bishop proposed to give upon such an auspicious occasion, but also the formal reply (in

Hungarian) which he suggested might be fitting for His Excellency the Archduke to read aloud in response.

'But you see, Károlyi,' the Archduke said (in German), 'this reply is all perfectly well and good, of course, except that the truth is my Hungarian is rather rusty. *Ich bin etwas heraus aus meinem Ungarisch*. So I'd be awfully obliged if you could take a look at it, and perhaps shorten and simplify it a bit.'

So Károlyi set to work. He cut. Then he cut some more. In the end he cut practically everything, until all that remained was: 'I am delighted to be here and have been greatly heartened by the things I have seen during the inspection' (*a tapasztaltakkal* in Hungarian).

The Archduke was extremely pleased with this shortened version.

They arrived, and after inspecting the Red Cross centre they were conducted to the County Hall, where a magnificent banquet had been prepared. Monsignor Schlauch delivered his eloquent speech, then the Archduke rose and took the shortened reply from his pocket.

'I am delighted to be here,' he read, 'and have been greatly heartened by the things I have seen during the tapa... the tapastapala.... the pastapatala...'

Seeing the difficulty their distinguished guest was in, the audience came to his rescue with a rousing cheer and a round of applause. The Archduke then shook hands with Monsignor Schlauch, and an escort of the city's leading citizens accompanied him to the railway station, whence he and Károlyi set off for Kolozsvár.

Károlyi sat alone in his compartment, cursing his thoughtlessness at leaving a word as difficult as *tapasztaltakkal* in the Archduke's speech. Not long after their departure, a servant knocked on the door to inform him that the Archduke wished to see him in his private carriage at his earliest convenience. Károlyi set off with a heavy heart, expecting a dressing down, but in fact the Archduke was in high spirits.

'I just wanted to thank you, Count Károlyi, for your wonderful little speech. That tricky word in particular seems to have really hit the spot. Definitely the *mot juste*, eh? That tapalapa, talapatata…oh, you know the one I mean! Absolute gem of a word!'

THE MONKEY

Every word of this account is true. In every particular it happened just as I relate, and I was intimately familiar with everyone involved. All are as I describe them, though I have chosen to conceal their identities: in the same way that at a masked ball one guest wears a *papier-mâché* nose, another a false beard, and another a toupée, so I have given the characters of this story different faces and names. Likewise, the real events did not actually take place in the city here named, nor perhaps even the same country, but somewhere else entirely. I am obliged to take this precaution because some of those here described may still be alive, though many have no doubt long since died. This is, after all, an old story, which took place about ten years before the First World War.

I was in Venice, on my way back from the Italian Riviera, and only intended to stop for a day or two. I ended up staying, however, for on the very first evening I was introduced to a woman of great beauty, whom the people of Venice called 'La Divina'. This was quite fitting, for there truly was something of the goddess in her, and she was not simply beautiful but in every regard entirely captivating.

There was an opera on at La Fenice and a friend I had happened to run into invited me to share a box with both him and La Divina. She was sitting facing the stage when I entered, and whether she was alone or with a friend I cannot recall: all I truly remember are those eyes.

They were huge, pale eyes of marbled grey. At first her face was in shadow—the performance having already begun—but when she turned to look at me those eyes caught the footlights' glow and sparkled with such bewitching splendour that I could barely muster a stammered greeting.

She invited me to visit her *palazzo* the next day.

I walked out of the box as though under a spell, and anyone seeing me as I staggered home must have thought I was blind drunk. That very night I wrote a sonnet in French about those beautiful eyes, though in truth I have never been much of a poet.

So I ended up staying. It was *Carnevale*, and there were balls and parties all over the city every night. La Divina invited me along to this or that acquaintance's house, so that before long I knew everyone. This also meant I was able to see her somewhere every evening.

But this story is not about me; I am simply trying to explain why I came to be spending so much time in Venetian society.

One particular party was hosted in the agreeable surroundings of the Palazzo Cornaro. The Principessa was the daughter of an American millionaire, while her husband was the last Prince Cornaro, that family which had once ruled over the Kingdom of Cyprus. Catharina Cornaro, however, bequeathed that island to the Republic of Venice in the middle of the sixteenth century, so it was perhaps not entirely appropriate for the *palazzo* to display the Cypriot coat of arms above both entrances, nor for the prince still to style himself a prince royal. (I should point out, incidentally, that I never actually met the Prince; he and the Principessa had lived apart, he in Naples and she in Venice, for many years.)

But that is by the by. The Princess, in any case, was very kind; she was also extraordinarily clever, and always seemed to be in a good mood. Guests who visited the palace for afternoon tea were always treated to the most artfully contrived little sandwiches, while the pastries were a melting, honeyed dream.

I soon became part of the Princess's more intimate circle, and often went over to play bridge in the evening. One of the stalwarts of this little circle was the local British consul, whom I will call MacBluff. He was a Scot, after all, and I think the name suits him: both at the card table and in his private life generally, he loved nothing better than a good bluff. His real name, of course, was completely different.

He was a strange fellow with a very dry sense of humour, and always seemed to be making fun not merely of others, but principally of himself. He was also extremely intelligent. From his appearance one would never have guessed that he was British, for he was a rather short, dark-haired man with high cheekbones and slightly slanted eyes which gave him an almost Tatar countenance. He assured me that such features were quite common among the Scots, and that many believe there to have been a tribe of Ural-Altaic nomads who migrated to Caledonia in some unrecorded era of prehistory, perhaps from the far north of Lapland.

'That, at least,' he added darkly, 'is what they say.'

His thick, black, wide-set eyebrows, hooded eyes and thin mouth always suggested that he was struggling to contain an outburst of laughter, but in fact he never laughed, and only very rarely smiled. All the same, something about his character endeared him to people, while his bridge style, which was both excellent and unpredictable, made him even more popular.

Everyone seemed to think him a little mad, and he certainly had his share of eccentricities. Perhaps the Foreign Office had sent him to Venice to get rid of him: after all, from an economic point of view, the Queen of the Adriatic had become at best a second-rate port. The southern Adriatic cities of Bari and Ancona saw much more commercial shipping, while Trieste handled virtually all the Austro-Hungarian

Empire's Mediterranean trade. Venice, meanwhile, was too narrow and shallow for modern freight vessels, and the lagoon had only two entrances of any consequence: the Lido and Malamocco canals. There is one more to the north, but even bringing a medium-sized barque through that gap is risky, while the Chioggia passage to the south is too far away to be practical. Sandbanks shift position in the open sea, and the lagoon itself is traversable only along narrow, winding channels. These too shift unpredictably, and if the guide posts are washed away or taken out, and if no pilot is available, a ship trying to navigate the channels is almost sure to run aground. That is why large ocean liners do not dock at the port of Venice, and the Regia Marina, the Italian Royal Navy, employs the military docks only for the smallest class of gunboat. Thus the city is protected not merely by the fortresses of the Lido, but also by its shifting maze of sandbanks.

All of which is to say that MacBluff was not a busy man, and had time to indulge his leisure pursuits. One of these was bug collecting. He had no interest in anything which scuttled upon the earth or flew through the air. Only creatures which lived in water, or more specifically in mud, caught his fancy, and he sought out those beetles and worms which populated the lagoon's oozy depths. It was this mud, and even the silt lining the city's many canals, that was his area of expertise, and one often saw him on some narrow waterway, scooping up handfuls of putrid slime with a long, ladle-shaped device of his own contrivance. His boat had a little desk on deck, where he would spread out what he had dredged from the bottom and examine it through a magnifying glass. Nothing he found appeared to disgust him, though it must have been rancid stuff: all of Venice's kitchen waste—and worse besides—ends up in the canals, and it is fortunate that frequent high tides sweep most of it out to sea. MacBluff, however, always conducted his experiments when the waters were at their lowest—and therefore foulest—but also, presumably, when his quarry was most abundant and easily found.

The Venetians, of course, had no idea what to make of all this, and called him '*l'inglese pazzo*', the mad Englishman.

Generally, however, he went out into the lagoon, sailing a little wooden skiff with a canvas sail. He always went alone, never inviting anyone to join him, and sometimes stayed out for two or three days at a stretch. He did everything himself, and must have been a first-rate sailor: he could navigate his boat down the narrowest and most indifferently marked channels, and I saw him out in winds which had his flat-bottomed boat heeling so far to leeward that I thought she must surely capsize. Perhaps he had spent time in the navy in his youth.

When I first met him he had been in Venice for about five years, but still spoke only English and French—both with a heavy Scots accent. He did not speak a word of Italian, and often said he 'wouldn't be seen dead speaking that ridiculous babble,' with a glower at anyone who looked likely to demur. 'It is a language,' he growled, 'fit only for larks and sparrows.'

He had other eccentricities besides bug collecting. He believed, for instance, in the transmigration of souls, and even claimed to remember each of his numerous reincarnations. He appeared to have lived through the most varied of historical epochs, but always in some humble or despised station. He had been a galley slave on a Byzantine warship, for instance, a Spanish hangman, and an English poacher in the days of Good Queen Bess, for which crime he had in turn been hanged. He told these tales in such a strange tone that it was impossible to say whether he was making fun of his listeners or of himself.

These reincarnations were again the topic of conversation on the evening I invited a young man by the name of Czobor as a guest to the Principessa's salon. He was a tall, slim youth with narrow shoulders, a long, thin nose and sloping forehead: the sort of distinguished countenance common among the most exalted members of the Austrian nobility. His hair was such a pale blonde he might almost have been albino, while his skin had the pallor of a pastel shirt too often and too vigorously laundered. His family, some of whom I knew well, had recommended him to me, and so I felt I had little choice but to bring him along on my visit to the Palazzo Cornaro.

MacBluff was explaining the principles of reincarnation, and reassuring us that he really could remember each of his past lives; even those in which he had been an animal. Yes, an animal! Everyone, he said, had once been an animal. He knew that for a fact.

Czobor, who was either offended in his religious beliefs by this contention, or else simply felt obliged to say something, cleared his throat.

'The human soul certainly is a great and impenetrable mystery...'

'An impenetrable mystery?' MacBluff boomed. 'Not a bit of it! Blazes, man, I even remember bumping into you in a previous life. Yes, you! You were a greyhound the colour of a bread roll.'

At this a great gust of laughter swept the room, so easy was it to imagine Czobor as a stately greyhound.

'And I'll tell you something else. You kept barking at me for no reason!' MacBluff went on.

'I...at you?'

'Yes, at me. Once you even chased me! If there hadn't been a good-sized tree nearby for me to clamber up then there's a good chance you'd have torn me to pieces. Because do you know what I was, eh? I was a monkey! Yes, a monkey! A monkey, man, a monkey!'

He glared at the young man with such ferocity that he seemed ready to kill him there and then if he dared so much as query this absurd statement. Only his eyebrows parted even wider than usual, and a quiver around the corners of his mouth suggested he was struggling to contain a laugh.

Many interrupted at once, saying come now, that was going a bit far and so on, but MacBluff refused to back down. With as much triumphant pride as if declaring himself the reincarnation of Julius Caesar or Alexander the Great, he bellowed the same words:

'Yes, that's right, a monkey! A monkey! A MONKEY!'

One of us, perhaps it was young Faliero, at last succeeded in moving the conversation on.

'Is the Honourable Consul really saying that all of us were animals in previous lives?'

'Certainly. You, for instance, were a tomcat, always prowling along some rooftop or other.'

Again, everybody laughed. Faliero's round face and bushy whiskers really did have something cat-like about them, but the barb here was still sharper, for it was rumoured that he had a habit of chasing after serving girls, who in Venice generally live in the attics.

I, meanwhile, was described as having been a peregrine falcon, but one which succeeded only in catching flies. Everyone was assigned a different animal ancestor, and each mordant word found its mark.

'And what about the ladies?' asked the stout, kindly Countess Pesaro. She was the head of a local charitable association, and though enormously good-hearted, there was no denying that at times she could be an insufferable busybody.

'Surely we were animals too. What about me, for instance? What was I?'

'My dear Countess, please don't insist. I can speak only the truth, and you are a lady of such distinction…'

'But I do insist! I certainly shan't take whatever you say amiss; after all, if you yourself were a monkey…'

A wicked gleam twinkled in MacBluff's eyes.

'Your Ladyship was a big white hen with a great many chicks, and every morning when you laid an egg there was a great commotion all through the poultry yard.'

A little taken aback, the Countess nonetheless forced a smile.

'I'm not sure I entirely understand, but I'm sure it's a very witty joke.'

Still, it was easy to see that she was hurt.

The American Principessa hurriedly interrupted.

'And me? You won't say anything about me?'

The Consul's face at once softened, as though abandoning all mockery.

'You? You were a very elegant little ermine, still in her brown summer coat. Such a coat is still valuable, of course, but not so valuable as in winter, when it turns pure white and is worth a living fortune. Nobody ever paid good money for a monkey's coat.'

This last sentence broke the tension which had been building around the table, and once more everybody laughed. Then we rose and the Principessa, myself, the plump Countess, MacBluff, and two descendants of a Venetian doge—called Fosco and Zen Foscari—all moved over to the card table. I sat next to the Principessa, who was a very imaginative player; it was always a pleasure to observe her style.

We sat down, but before the first hand could be dealt, MacBluff turned to the Countess.

'Did you know that I visited Venice in another life, in the middle of the seventh century?'

'As a monkey, perhaps?' asked the Countess. Though a very kindly woman, she still had not quite forgiven the business about the chicken.

'No, as a Greek galley slave. But at that time the city was somewhere else entirely. I remember it all very clearly; there were already a few buildings on the Rialto, but most of the houses were then much closer to *terra firma*. There was a raised sandbank in the wetlands around Mestre, stretching out towards Torcello. The whole area is shallow lagoon now.'

'Really? How do you mean?'

This had thoroughly piqued everyone's curiosity.

'Just as I say. I remember it all quite distinctly.'

He began to tell his tale, speaking so convincingly that everyone gathered round to hear. There was no prospect of a card game now.

The Principessa shot me a knowing smile, as if to say, 'Isn't the poor man off his rocker?' but my impression was rather that everything he said seemed to have a calculated purpose. Was he trying to make us forget that we had been the victims of his mockery at the dinner table?

He was, in any case, a marvellous raconteur, and seemingly off the cuff, he wove a complex and involving story. The galley slaves, he told us, had risen up in revolt against their cruel masters, slaying their guards and taking control of the ship. They then offered their services in defence of the young republic, and he gave a minute description of the size, location and appearance of the city in those days. He described everything so persuasively, with such ardour and so many arresting details, that all conversation ceased. All of us, the local Venetians in particular, were spellbound, and we drew ever closer to him. Perhaps these proud natives hoped to hear the name of some ancestor in the Consul's description. He sketched a map on a sheet of paper as he spoke.

'The harbour was here, and there was a little wooden fort on an island just here. This was the central island in those days, but there was another settlement out here...'

The pencil flew across the page in quick, confident strokes. It was only a small sheet of paper, however, and soon he had run out of room. The Countess turned to the Principessa.

'Darling, you wouldn't have someone bring us some more paper? I do like to see where everything used to be.'

MacBluff closed his eyes and I had the impression he was rapidly calculating something, or weighing two possible courses of action. Then he spoke.

'Please, don't bother, anything I can sketch here will be of no use. Still, if you really are curious, Countess, I'd be happy to bring a few drawings I've already prepared of old Venice. They're not entirely accurate, of course; it's been almost a millennium and a half since I saw these things, after all, and that is a considerable span of time. Still, they should give you some impression of the place. I drew them immediately after my arrival in Venice, five years ago. The memory was so vivid then that I sat down that very first evening and put what I had seen to paper. That very first evening! I worked on them right through the night!'

He spoke with such apparent seriousness that it was impossible to say whether he was making fun of us or really believed what he said. There was only the faintest trace of mockery in his voice.

Countess Pesaro was extremely grateful, having long since forgotten the earlier offence. When they said goodnight, the hand she offered him to kiss was extended with genuine warmth. The other Venetians also said that they would be present without fail the following day. Everyone was filled with curiosity, quite forgetting how self-evidently absurd the whole business was. Then the card game at last began, with MacBluff bidding three spades in the very first hand.

The next morning we all reassembled and MacBluff presented his drawings of 'seventh-century Venice'. There were four or five of them, if I remember correctly, each about half a metre across, mounted on metal plates and framed behind glass. All displayed strikingly fine draughtsmanship, with some lines lightly accentuated in Indian ink, and pale washes of watercolour. The sea was aquamarine, the islands light green. As in many old maps, the perspective adopted was the so-called bird's-eye view, from an imagined position above and oblique to the city. All had been drawn with such marvellous skill that it was obvious only someone with both talent and experience could have produced them. Even the channels of the lagoon were sketched with pencil lines, while the depth of the water was indicated through lighter and darker shades of blue. Abhorring a vacuum, ancient cartographers used to decorate those empty spaces of open ocean with sea monsters and caravels. Here, by contrast, little marsh beetles scuttled across the blank spaces of the map, and mud worms threw up spirals of wet sand.

This was all both novel and unexpected, while the 'Monkey' himself also showed a hitherto unseen side to his complex personality.

'All done in one night! The first night! Right through to morning! I was in a trance, just as though I had been hypnotised!' His eyes gleamed as he spoke.

Why did he so insist on this? Probably to increase the admiration of the Venetians still further. At the time I thought no more than that he was clearly a man of great artifice, and that I did not believe a single word he said. Certainly those drawings were so fine, so detailed, that even one of them must have required a minimum of two or three days' solid work, and more likely four or five. A discerning eye might also have noticed, despite the protective sheets of glass, that all these drawings were on copy paper. Though the craftsmanship was superb, still it was possible to see— and the material confirmed it—that these were not the original drawings but copies.

What a strange fellow, I thought, putting such enormous effort into a prank like this. That, however, was precisely what struck me as so curious. Why would he claim this to be the product of a few hours' work when it so patently could not be the case? I do not believe, however, that anyone else present thought to doubt his story. They were filled only with admiration, eagerly devouring the 'authentic facts' of early Venice which MacBluff regaled them with. This should come as no surprise, for whether what he told us was true or false, it was certainly fascinating. He must have had great knowledge of that period, as well as of the broader historical background, for his talk had an almost tangible vividness which seduced even me.

This performance lasted for a long time; the Consul never tired, and the more he spoke, the happier he seemed to grow. He was clearly delighted to have an audience, and his eyes glowed like coals.

When at last his talk came to an end and he was putting away his pictures, the 'mother hen' approached him with a winning smile.

'I have a very great favour to ask,' she began, then faltered; she was clearly embarrassed, and even blushed, before mustering the courage to ask the Consul whether he could have one of the pictures—the one showing an overview of the city and surrounding lagoon 'in its original state'—copied for her.

'I would so love to have a copy, and to frame it as nobly as it deserves! I have some mosaic frames, for instance, which would suit the period, and I could hang it above my bed, next to the picture of Our Saviour!'

'My dear Countess, I am ever at your service. But why copy it? After all, I don't need this, since I only drew what I saw in my memory. I've barely even looked at it since. Please, accept it as a gift!'

He lifted the drawing in question out of the case and handed it to her. This gave the matronly Countess Pesaro such pleasure that she only managed with difficulty to restrain herself from throwing her arms about the Scotsman's neck and covering him with kisses.

All the strangeness which I have so far related, and everything which seemed either pointless or inexplicable in the 'Monkey's' conduct, was to this point only a series of fleeting impressions. My life among the Venetian *beau monde*, and my pursuit of La Divina, occupied me so completely that I had little leisure to ponder MacBluff's strange conduct. Only that silent archivist who resides within all of us, keeping a record of our lives' manifold little occurrences, thought to file these memories away in a drawer, together with the other connected characters.

It was perhaps a week or so later when I received some unexpected news. Three days earlier MacBluff had abruptly left Venice.

He was gone, seemingly for good.

He did not bid anyone farewell, nor even so much as telephone. He told nobody, and did not even take the trouble to cancel lunch or dinner engagements for the coming week, as any half-civilised person would have done. There was not a single goodbye, not even to Principessa Cornaro. Nobody.

Vanished, like a puff of smoke!

This was a source of great surprise and consternation. What could possibly have motivated such churlish behaviour? That was when the aforementioned mental archivist reminded me of two previously overlooked occurrences.

I had at the time a habit of going out into the lagoon by gondola, towards Murano, Torcello or even Burano, where I once accompanied La Divina to the local lace-making workshop. On such trips I sometimes saw MacBluff's little skiff in a side-channel, but at the time I thought nothing of it.

One day I chartered a small sailing boat for San Francesco del Deserto. I have known this little island at the northern extremity of the lagoon for many years, and am extremely fond of it. In the garden of its little monastery stands a cypress tree which is taller and broader in girth than any other I have seen in my life. The pious monks claim that Saint Francis himself drove his staff into the ground there, and from it grew the tree.

The wind having shifted, we took a different route back, and I soon spotted MacBluff's skiff lying at anchor not far off.

'Aha!' I said to myself. 'Out hunting beetles again, are we? I think I shall pay you a visit.'

I told the skipper to bring us alongside, but MacBluff came out from beneath his canvas awning in a rage, shouting at us in Italian.

'What do you want? What business have you got here?'

Seeing me, his tone abruptly shifted, and he went on in English.

'Ah, it's you! What are you doing here?'

'I just thought I'd drop by,' I said lightly, 'and take a look at this fine vessel of yours.'

I was already preparing to clamber across, but he stood in front of me, then sat down on the only free space where I might have come aboard, between the mast and the canvas awning.

'I wouldn't recommend it: the old girl is in a filthy state!' Then he changed the subject. 'Where are you coming from? And what brought you all the way out here?'

It was as though some hint of wary suspicion glinted for a moment in his eyes.

I told him we had just come from San Francesco.

'San Francesco? Splendid little place, isn't it? I'm sure you had a wonderful time. Now if you don't mind, I've got work to be getting on with…'

We sailed on. Still, I had two fresh mysteries to consider. One was the little metal tube I had noticed poking through a hole in the skiff's canvas shelter. It was a couple of centimetres in diameter, rather like the muzzle on one of those heavy punt guns they occasionally use on duck shoots. If you fire one of those at a big flock you can sometimes bring down ten or twenty birds with a single shot. Might he be doing a bit of shooting out in the quiet of the lagoon? The fact is, though, you rarely see anything besides seagulls out there. The other peculiar thing was his shouting at us in Italian, when he always made such a fuss about not speaking it. Then again, they were only the sort of expressions that everyone picks up in a foreign country, whether they try to or not.

This had happened perhaps a month or so before he disappeared, but the second incident took place just a day or two before, and became more interesting in light of what followed.

I had gone out to the littoral of Sant'Erasmo, which is to the north of the Lido and much broader; here there are vegetable gardens and orchards which stretch right down to the water's edge. I knew the place relatively well from a previous visit in summertime, when the pomegranate trees were in bloom and everything was beautiful. I had visited several times in boyhood as well, and even painted a few watercolours of the place when I still called myself a painter. Now it was winter, but I knew of a gardener on the island who grew wonderful hyacinths in greenhouses, right through the year. The city flower shops only had a few left, but I wanted to send a big bouquet to the Albrizzis, who had invited me to lunch on several occasions.

Reaching Sant'Erasmo, I set off in the direction of the gardener's cottage. That was when I saw the Consul, standing about fifty metres up ahead and talking to a man in work overalls. They were facing one another, and the Consul was speaking with big, expansive gestures. He was evidently explaining something, and laughing at the same time. That was the first time I ever saw the 'Monkey' laugh. I had hardly taken a couple of paces towards them when they saw me, and the unknown man at once disappeared behind a trellis of haricot beans. MacBluff waited for me alone.

Greeting me warmly, he asked me what brought me to Sant'Erasmo. I said that I had come to see the famous gardener.

'Och, isn't he fantastic!' he said enthusiastically. 'I was looking for him too, but I got lost. I was just asking that fellow for directions.'

He then gave a very circumstantial—perhaps too circumstantial—account of how he had happened upon a local labourer who had spent some years in America, and so could communicate in English.

'A stroke of luck, eh? You know I don't understand a word of this Italian twittering. Not a blessed word of it!'

We walked together to the gardener's cottage, where MacBluff bought practically the entire shop. I had to interpret for him, and to tell him the price of everything, since he professed not to understand even the numbers. This ignorance too seemed a trifle overdone, and together with his lively conversation with the apparently English-speaking man in workman's overalls, gave rise to a quiet suspicion that this too was one of MacBluff's little games. But why pretend not to speak Italian? Here, as elsewhere, I could see no logic to the man's behaviour.

These were the two memories which arose in my mind when I heard of MacBluff's unexpected disappearance.

Then, about three days after that, I bumped into Foscari near the church of San Moisè. He took me by the arm, saying that we should go into the church to talk. I had no idea what he wanted, but followed him inside. After looking around to make sure that we were truly alone, he turned to me with a nervous whisper.

'Haven't you heard? But of course not; you're a foreigner! The whole thing is a damned unpleasant mess! Faliero, Zen and I were all summoned to the police headquarters on account of the MacBluff business. What? You didn't know about that either? The national security people came here on the trail of a spy, and interrogated us about his maps. Then they went to Countess Pesaro's too, and took away the drawing he gave her. It turns out that the houses, churches and so on were nothing but decoys, while the little bugs and worms are drawn exactly where the forts are sited! The channels were also marked precisely, as was every sandbank and shallow in the whole lagoon! It's an absolute nightmare! Who would have believed that this bug-hunting business was all just a charade, and that MacBluff spent years charting every inch of the lagoon, right under our noses? The channels in and out of the naval port are top secret! And what a lot of rubbish he spouted, about the transmigration of souls and old Venice and remembering his previous life as a monkey! Then here in the city he would scoop out big spoonfuls of mud in front of everyone, so that we'd all laugh at him and think him a mad fool! It's outrageous, and we all just laughed!'

Foscari went on in this vein for a long time, and it was evident that what mortified him most was the idea that they, the cunning, clever Italians, had been so thoroughly outwitted by an *inglese*.

The national security services performed a thorough search of MacBluff's private apartment, and confiscated everything they found. This led to a diplomatic incident, since while consuls, unlike ambassadors, were not officially extraterritorial persons, it was a generally observed courtesy to treat them as such. The storm quickly blew over, however, and it never made the newspapers in either country.

Nobody ultimately came out of the affair any the worse, except perhaps the kind-hearted mother hen, the Countess Pesaro, whose beautifully framed drawing of 'seventh-century Venice', of which she was so proud, was taken away and never returned.

MacBluff was later transferred to Bern. Years later, during the war, I heard that from this neutral territory he had succeeded in organising a surprise bombing raid on the Zeppelin works near Friedrichshafen, on the shores of Lake Constance.

The 'Monkey', after all, was a crafty fellow!

Notes

Danse Macabre

1. Most of the characters in this story are historical figures. The 'famously handsome Count Dillon' is probably Édouard Dillon (1751–1839), gentleman in waiting to the Comte d'Artois, whose daughter Georgine married the Hungarian nobleman Lajos Károlyi, great-grandfather of Bánffy's relative Mihály Károlyi (see Note 18).

Lememame

2. When this story was written (1915), Munkács was part of Greater Hungary. It is now Mukachevo, Ukraine.

3. István Tisza, Prime Minister of Hungary from 1913–17. Initially an opponent of war, he became persuaded to support the conflict on the grounds that Hungary should not jeopardise her alliance with Germany. He personally served on the Italian front.

4. Today's Lviv, Ukraine.

5. The towns and villages of this story are all real places in the Mezőség (In Romanian, Câmpia Transilvaniei), a largely treeless region of rolling hills to the east of Kolozsvár (Cluj-Napoca). It was an area that Bánffy knew and loved and it features in many of his writings. Mezőbányica, Lememame's village, is present-day Băița. Later in the story Bánffy mentions

Dedrád (in Romanian, Dedrad), Szászrégen (Reghin) and Teke (Teaca).

6. The gendarmes are the dreaded *csendőrök*, a quasi-military provincial police force charged with maintaining public order and in the popular imagination notorious for their primitive methods and brutality.

7. Bikal in Romanian is Bicălatu. The fact that Bánffy specifies that the soldier from this village was a Hungarian is probably accurate. In 1910, five years before this story was written, Bikal's population is recorded as being ninety-five percent Hungarian and figures from 2011 show that it still retains its Hungarian majority. Mezőbányica/Băiţa, on the other hand, is majority Romanian, as it presumably was in Bánffy's day too.

Wolves

8. This story is set in 1785, following an uprising known as the Revolt of Horea, Cloşca and Crişan. The direct causes of this uprising were connected to a dispute over army recruitment but beneath the surface lay discontent at the marginalisation of the Orthodox Vlach (or Romanian) serfs who made up a large part of Transylvania's population. The rebels principally attacked landed interests, aiming to overthrow feudalism, dismantle the nobility and create a new, egalitarian society. The revolt was swiftly and brutally put down (Horea and Cloşca were broken on the wheel in Gyulafehérvár/Alba Iulia and Crişan took his own life in prison). Transylvania at this

date was ruled from Habsburg Austria as part of Hungary though it was home to many ethnic groups. 'Vlach' is a term that was widely used until the late 19th century for Romanian speakers across eastern and southeastern Europe. The name derives from the province of Wallachia, which merged with Moldavia in 1860 to form the Kingdom of Romania. We have retained Bánffy's use of the term here because 'Romanian' could be construed as anachronistic in this eighteenth-century context.

9. The 'Majesty' here is the Habsburg emperor Joseph II.

10. Komondor: a breed of dog with an off-white coat forming long corkscrewing locks.

The Infected Planet

11. The narrator is thinking of towns and villages in the Mezőség, Bánffy's homeland, where the story 'Lememame' is also set (see Note 5). As so often, Bánffy uses the Hungarian toponyms. The Romanian name for Mezőbánd is Band and Mócs is Mociu.

12. *The Tragedy of Man* (*Az ember tragédiája*) is a verse play by Imre Madách, written in 1861. One of the great classics of Hungarian literature, it follows Adam, the archetypal man, from his creation through the various ages of history and achievement, into space and the future. It is a strangely prescient work in some ways—as is this story of Bánffy's, which seems to prefigure not only the destruction of WWII (it

was written in 1939), but also the despoliation of the planet and the dominance of mankind in an age which Sir David Attenborough has termed the 'Anthropocene epoch'.

Somewhere

13. Bánffy is being disingenuous. It soon becomes clear (from the professor's Hungarian surname, for example, and from the Hungarian theatre that the characters attend) that this story is set in his homeland of Transylvania, after the Treaty of Trianon (signed in 1920 after the First World War) had ceded the entire region to Romania. Bánffy wrote this story at a time when his own life had 'utterly, utterly changed'. His sentences about the need to explain whether a familiar place name 'encompasses an area broader or narrower than it once did. Expanded or contracted' are not as throwaway as he pretends. He is thinking of the changes brought about in Central and Eastern Europe—and to Hungary in particular—by the wholesale re-drawing of borders after the collapse of the Austro-Hungarian Empire. His own family home was among those transferred to the newly enlarged state of Romania and he was permitted to occupy a room in his former town house in Kolozsvár/Cluj. There are certain interesting parallels between this story and Bánffy's later *Transylvanian Trilogy*, but readers familiar to both will detect in this earlier work (written only a few years after Trianon) a much bitterer and more unreconciled tone.

Talking Nothing

14. Elected Prince of Transylvania in 1661, Mihály Apafi was the last ruler of Transylvania under the suzerainty of the Ottomans. When they were defeated at Vienna in 1683 and then expelled from Buda in 1686, their power in the region was replaced by the Habsburgs, who were less amenable to Transylvanian autonomy. Mihály Apafi is remembered as an easy-going man, not greatly addicted to statecraft, a lover of food and wine. He introduced tobacco to Transylvania.

15. The reference is to the Hungarian Uprising of 1848–9, which turned into bitter armed conflict against Austria. Under the military commander Artúr Görgei (born Görgey as Bánffy spells it, though he himself changed the final y to an i on the grounds that it looked less aristocratic), Hungary won significant victories and in the end it was only with Russian help that Austria succeeded in defeating Hungary. In August 1849 Görgey was faced with the ignominious task of surrendering unconditionally. His decision to do so—based on the belief that to continue fighting would bring a bitterer defeat and worse reprisals—led to widespread accusations of treason in Hungarian patriotic circles. Világos, where the surrender took place, is now Șiria, close to the Romanian-Hungarian border. The Bohus manor, where the armistice was signed, still stands.

16. Today's Oradea, Romania.

17. Torda is now Turda and the river Aranyos the Arieș.

Segesvár is Sighișoara. The Küküllő river is the Târnava Mare.

18. Count Mihály Károlyi (1875–1955), Bánffy's cousin, was a pacifist and political radical who came to power at the head of his National Council in 1918. Known as the 'Red Count', he voluntarily divided up and redistributed his own estates. Political pressures forced his resignation in the spring of 1919, when Hungary declared itself a Communist republic.

Published in Hungary
Felelős kiadó a Somerset Kiadó és Tanácsadó Kft. ügyvezető igazgatója
1136 Budapest, Pannónia u. 11.
Szerkesztő: Annabel Barber
Nyomdai előkészítés: Kuzmich Anikó
Nyomta és kötötte TJ Books, Anglia
ISBN 978-1-905131-90-7